DIAMOND SOLITAIRE

DIAMOND SOLITAIRE

A DIAMOND RING DARK ROMANCE

THE KIDNAPPED SERIES
BOOK 1

ALIX KEY

DIAMOND
FREEPORT PRESS

Published by Diamond Freeport Press
P.O. Box 42133, Arlington, VA 22204

ISBN 978-1-95018-478-1

Discover other titles by Alix Key at www.alixkey.com

091625ak

ALSO BY ALIX KEY

Find a complete, up-to-date list of Alix's books at www.alixkey.com.

The Kidnapped Series

Diamond Solitaire

Rough Diamond

Conflict Diamond

Priceless Diamond

The Irish Mob Trilogy

Irish Brute

Irish Vice

Irish Reign

The Boston Mob Trilogy

Her Irish Savage

Her Irish Protector

Her Irish King

The Taming the Mob Princess Trilogy

Taken Enemy

Twisted Enemy

Tamed Enemy

The Sinful Mafia Series

Sinful Mafia Santa

Sinful Mafia Deception

Sinful Mafia Seduction

Sinful Mafia Salvation

WORD OF WARNING

Diamond Solitaire **is a dark romance.**

It contains hard-to-read scenes, graphic language, and explicit sexual content.

A complete list of potential triggers can be found at:

https://alixkey.com/books/kidnapped-series/

Please don't read this book if you are sensitive to any of those triggers. But if you believe in the redemptive power of love to overcome near-unimaginable trauma, then this is the book for you.

Welcome to the Diamond Ring.

1

ALIX

SOMETIMES LOVING SOMEONE MEANS YOU WANT TO KILL THEM.

My brother was supposed to meet me on campus an hour ago. Late lunch, just the two of us. Twins united against the world because we turn twenty-six today. I even wore my favorite skirt, the one with daisies on it.

But Leo stood me up.

He isn't using again. He can't be.

He swears he was fired from Barney's Grill last month because some niece or cousin or long-lost goddaughter needed a job waiting tables. He promises he'll find something else soon, any day now.

So why wasn't he waiting for me outside Barton Library?

Maybe we got our wires crossed. Maybe he's upstairs in our tiny apartment, fidgeting on the sway-backed couch that doubles as his bed. Maybe he forgot to charge his phone; that's why he didn't answer my texts. Didn't pick up when I called.

He was fiddling with his dark-blue chip this morning,

tapping the plastic against the lip of his coffee mug. He got the Narcotics Anonymous token at his meeting last week, marking six months of sobriety.

He isn't using. He can't be using.

I slam my keycard against the ancient entry pad for the third time, finally finding the sweet spot that makes the release buzz. Pushing open the heavy glass door, I step into a lobby that smells like day-old pizza and sweat. I cross to the line of mailboxes and force my key into the gritty lock. The key cuts into my palm, but it finally turns.

Nothing. No birthday cards. No slips telling me to pick up a package at the post office. Not even a coupon pack from every sorry business with a storefront on the south side of Dover, Delaware.

The elevator wheezes like the June heat has melted something important in its gears and cables, but it shudders me up to the fifth floor. For just a second, with my key set to turn the deadbolt, I wonder if Leo has a surprise waiting inside.

Maybe he's made up with our father. Or our stepmother. Maybe this is all a major Step Nine—NA's instruction to make amends—and every one of the family members and friends who've cut me off for trusting my twin is waiting to shout "Surprise!" before singing "Happy birthday, dear Alix-and-Leo."

I shoulder the door open, pushing hard when it sticks in the June humidity. Of course the apartment's empty. The hot afternoon air hasn't stirred for hours.

"Leo?" I ask anyway, because I want to be wrong.

Silence.

He isn't using. He can't be using.

I loop my heavy hair into a loose knot and cross to the scratched coffee table, looking for something to use as a fan. Three books are stacked there: *Clinical Textbook of Addictive Disorders*, *Individual Psychodynamic Psychotherapy*, and *Neuroimaging in Addiction*. They match two dozen other books stacked on the shaky nightstand in my bedroom. Finishing my dissertation is the only thing left between me and my PhD. I'm through taking classes at Sherman University, through teaching them as well.

A bright white corner of paper peeks out from beneath the largest book. I ease it free, hoping I can use it to fan dry the sweat prickling at the base of my throat.

Bright red letters glare from the top of the page: EVICTION NOTICE.

In black, below: "To tenants Alix Key and Leo Key, all other residents, and unnamed occupants at..."

"...tenancy is hereby terminated due to non-payment of rent..."

"...required to quit and vacate the subject premises..."

"...thirty (30) day legal notice..."

"...midnight cancellation of electronic access to premises..."

"...dated: May 21..."

I reread the page three times, like the words might change if I stare at them long enough. Leo must have gotten the notice a month ago. He's hidden it for the past thirty days.

But at midnight tonight, my keycard turns into a pumpkin. I'm out on my ear, along with my brother and every last stick of the broken-down furniture around me.

He's using. He has to be using again.

2

ALIX

I WANT THERE TO BE SOME MISTAKE.

Leo moved in six months ago, the day I picked him up from Spring Valley Renewal Center in a rented Honda. We celebrated with Oreo Blizzards before I dropped him off at St. Bart's for his first NA meeting—ninety meetings in ninety days.

Three months ago, red chip shiny on his sweaty palm, he asked if he could drop off our rent check at the landlord's office, halfway between our apartment and Leo's job at Barney's Grill. He promised a receipt. I could follow behind him, watch him every step of the way. He begged to be trusted. To help with something, anything.

I love him.

He's my brother.

My twin.

I *did* follow him the first time, staying far enough back that he didn't see me, even though he looked over his shoulder every ten steps or so. But he brought me a receipt, signed and dated.

And he was so, so proud. He kept going to meetings every day, even though he had his red chip, even though he'd done his ninety.

Now, I carry the eviction notice into my bedroom. I put it on top of my psych books as I wrestle open the drawer of my nightstand. It sticks in the mid-summer humidity, but I'm persistent. I fumble beneath my nail scissors and my hand lotion, shove aside a handful of cough drops and a tube of cherry-flavor ChapStick.

The receipts should be here. I keep them as proof of payment because I'm the responsible one.

They're gone. Which makes me pretty sure they were never any good. Leo forged them or photocopied them or…I don't even know how else he could come up with fakes.

"Dammit, Leo…" My words bake in the stifling room.

I don't have the money to pay three months rent, even if I can reach our landlord before midnight. I *had* a grad student stipend, funds that were supposed to get me through my doctorate. It ended when I finished winter quarter, when I stopped taking classes and teaching. Knowing I'd be "ABD"—all but dissertation—I'd planned, saved a little. But I'd counted on Leo's wages from the restaurant.

I have two hundred dollars in my bank account. Another forty in my wallet, if…

I dig my wallet out of my frayed backpack.

My student ID is there. My driver's license too. I don't carry credit cards—for so many years they weren't safe, not when Leo was using. I scissor open the bill slot with my fingers.

Empty.

He took my change, too, even my lucky Eleanor Roosevelt quarter.

Anger feels like a live animal chewing its way out of my belly. But I'm embarrassed too. Ashamed that—once again—everyone else was right. Leo has betrayed me.

I'm going to be sick. I run to the bathroom and lean over the toilet, retching and choking, but nothing comes up. I give up and go back to my bedroom, collapsing on the edge of my sagging bed.

My heartbeat pounds in my ears. My numb fingers take a while to figure out how to get my phone out of my skirt pocket. They take even longer to text my dad, using full sentences because that's the kind of thing he likes.

> Sorry to reach out this way, but I've fallen behind on rent. Any chance I can borrow $1000?

Three dots float, and I allow myself to breathe. But the dots disappear and five minutes later there's still no reply.

Fine. I'll text Aunt Cindy, my mother's sister.

> Alix here—sorry it's been so long. Long story but my stipend's run out, and I still have a month or two before my dissertation's done. If I could borrow $1000, I'll pay you back in two months. With interest, of course.

I add a smiley face and tap send. The message flashes Delivered, then Read. But there aren't any dots, and five minutes later I'm reaching out to my stepsisters.

Olivia first. Then Ava. I'm waiting for answers when the screen turns to black broken by angry white letters. Wicked Stepmother is calling.

It seemed funny when I put her in my contacts under that name. And it's not like she'll ever see my screen. Still, my stomach executes a triple axel before I tap the green icon. "Candace!" I say, stretching my lips into a fake smile to keep my voice bright.

"You know the rules."

"But it's been so long—"

"No calling or texting from you or Leo."

"Leo's not even here!"

"We can't help you anymore. We won't."

"I just—"

"Not your father. Not your aunt. Not your stepsisters. You made your choice, Alix. Now you have to live with the consequences. Don't bother calling again. Everyone just blocked you."

A crash on her end tells me she slammed down her landline.

I clutch my phone, desperately swiping through my contacts. It's been years since I added a new name. There's a handful of entries for friends from high school. Maybe a dozen from college. Only one from grad school, because by then I'd learned the truth—Leo ruins everything.

He takes and he takes and he takes, and one by one, each of my friends had enough. It wasn't Leo's using, they said. It was me, standing by him. Enabling him.

I try to swallow the red-green taste of enraged shame as I stare at my last possible lifeline: Jason Carter. We met my first week of grad school at Sherman. He was my first—my only—boyfriend. We dated for three and a half years. The last time he was in this apartment was Thanksgiving, eight months ago.

Leo showed up three hours late, stumbling into the rickety kitchen table as he lost his balance. He shattered a thrift-store bowl because he thought the cranberry sauce was blood, then he threw our turkey off the fire escape to protect us from supposed poison.

Jason was a saint. Together, we talked Leo down. We got him to stop shouting, to stop sobbing, to—finally—fall asleep in my bed.

And when Jason asked if he could see me the next night, I thought he was finally going to propose. We'd worked so well together. We'd shared so much.

He wanted to meet at Ondine's, the little bistro where we had our first date. I braved the Black Friday sales in Dover for a killer outfit—little black dress, matching bra and panties that made me blush, and actual high heels—the only ones I'd ever owned.

His eyes went wide when I walked in the door. He waved off the waitress when she came to take our drinks order, and I waited for him to reach into his pocket, to bring out a ring. Instead, he took my hand and said, "Alix, these are the hardest words I've ever said. But I can't stay with you, not if Leo's in your life. He's an addict. A user."

"He's going to a meeting tomorrow!" I said. "He feels terrible about last night."

"He always feels terrible. And nothing ever changes. How many times has he been to rehab?"

Six. No, seven. But I said, "This time is different. He'll do it for *us*. For you and me."

Jason shook his head. "I'm sorry," he said, and he *did* sound sorry. "We both know that's not enough. So there can't be an 'us.'" He stood and pushed his chair in very carefully. "I'm sorry," he said again and left, just as the waitress came back to the table.

So, yeah. I can't call Jason. I jam my phone back into my pocket.

I'm livid about Leo. Desperate. He's lied to me more times than I can count. Cheated. Stolen.

But I can't give up on him. He's my brother. My *twin*.

When we were babies, we slept in one crib. We spoke our own private language before we spoke English. We still finish each other's sentences, and it's freaky the number of times I take out my phone, knowing he's about to call.

When our mother died, he was the only one who understood why I couldn't cry. And at the wedding reception when Dad married Candace, Leo slipped me a miniature voodoo doll dressed like our stepmother, complete with half a dozen straight pins.

We started at University of Delaware at the same time. I flirted with anorexia my first semester, trying to make it through an entire day of classes on an apple and eleven raw cashews because calories seemed easier to control than my impossible freshman classes. He made me go to Student Counseling, where I got better and fell in love with psychology.

But by the time I was ready to thank him, he'd found drugs.

It started with Ritalin his roommate gave him—enough to get a buzz and study all night long. Adderall got him through first semester exams. The first time he took meth seemed like a big deal, but soon he was hooked, with ecstasy and ketamine and God knew what else on the side.

I should have been there for him, the way he was there for me. But I wasn't. So I tried to make it up by staying loyal, even when it cost me my friends, my family, even the man I thought I'd marry.

Now Leo's rewarded me by getting us evicted.

I have two hundred dollars in the bank. I have no clue where I'm going to live. No one to turn to. Nowhere to go.

I'm so angry, my fingers shake as I text Leo.

> Call me, buttface

> Now

> Don't be a baby

But he doesn't call, and he doesn't text back.

And suddenly, I can't stand the idea of being in the apartment anymore. It's too hot. The walls are too close. I'm too furious.

I haven't had a drink since Leo got out of Spring Valley. I've been supporting his sobriety, trying to make it easier. Make him stronger.

My mouth is suddenly full of saliva, like I've already taken a huge gulp of a lemon drop martini. I swallow hard as I yank open my closet door.

I'm tired of saying *no*. *No* to drinks. *No* to friends and relatives who say Leo's a disaster. *No* to my thesis advisor who wants to know if I'm close to finishing my dissertation. *No* to the crazy voice deep inside my skull that says I should walk away from Dover, from Sherman U, from Leo, from *everything*, and just start over.

But tonight…

Tonight I'm celebrating my birthday. Tonight *no* isn't part of my vocabulary. Tonight I'm saying *yes* to every opportunity that crosses my path.

3

ALIX

~

YES IS HARD FOR ME TO SAY.

I'll never tell a living soul, but I'm broken. I've tried touching myself *down there* since Jason left. I thought maybe I could do on my own what never happened with him.

Nothing.

I know enough psychology to be certain my brain is the problem. I've created a terrible feedback loop: I don't respond sexually, so I worry about ever being able to respond, which stresses me out, so I don't respond sexually.

At this point, I can't even make myself think real words—clinical ones *or* slang ones. *Down there* is the most I can manage, and that leaves me feeling embarrassed. Ashamed.

I'm a mess.

I want *yes* to be my ticket out of this vicious circle.

I don't know if I feel light-headed because my brother has pulled the rug out from under me or because the apartment is hotter than Hades' left armpit or because I've decided to spend my last two hundred dollars on cocktails in some bar trying to solve the problem of my broken body. I need to put together some vaguely appropriate outfit, but first I manhandle the window in my bedroom, punching the sash with the heel of my hand until it finally shrieks and slides open.

A lazy breeze drifts in and I immediately feel a thousand times better. I stick my head outside and gulp fresh air like this is my last day of freedom. I don't even mind that heat radiates off the iron fire escape.

It's midsummer eve, the summer solstice, so the sun won't set for a few hours. Leo and I used to love celebrating our birthday on the longest day of the year—it makes it last even longer, Leo used to say.

Forget about Leo!

At least for tonight.

Before I can pull back into my room and start ransacking my closet, a squawk shreds the air and a massive crow lands on the fire escape. As he shifts from foot to foot, tilting his head for a better view of me, he's joined by three of his buddies.

I laugh, because the last week has been full of long days at the library. I haven't seen my bird friends since last weekend, but they haven't forgotten me. I reach for a jar that I keep on my nightstand and unscrew the lid, taking out a handful of shelled, unsalted peanuts.

"Hello, Gorgeous," I say to the first crow, placing a peanut on my windowsill.

He hops over to collect my gift before I have a chance to step back. Gorgeous flies off, but the other birds approach, bobbing their heads as I greet them by name—Nosy and Grabby and Caw—and give them their own treats. The birds make short work of their nuts, craning their necks as they search for more.

It's my birthday, and my black-feathered friends are the only ones who'll share my celebration. I'm about to duck back inside to grab another handful of peanuts when Gorgeous returns.

His wings flap wide as he settles on the fire escape. When he tilts his head, I see something in his beak. "What's that, Gorgeous?" I ask.

He hops over to my window, as if he understands every word I say. Ducking his head with perfect precision, he drops his prize on the sill. He retreats to his fellow crows, but he cranes his neck, pointing to the gift and fluffing his feathers with pride.

I pick up the present and turn it to catch a better angle in the sunlight. It's a battered metal heart, the kind a careful owner puts on their dog's collar, with a name and a phone number so a lost animal can find its way home. The heart used to be red, but it's so beat-up, I can't make out any of the letters or numbers engraved on its surface.

Closing my fingers around the charm, I nod gravely to Gorgeous. "Thank you," I say, and I'm surprised that tears thicken my words.

Before I can say anything else, my little murder of crows takes flight. I watch them fly toward the park, one block over. When they're gone, I turn to take stock of my closet. It's not like I have a fairy godmother. I have to make do with whatever I already own.

I have a pair of pencil skirts and a trio of tops, the ones I wore when I taught. I have the never-worn bridesmaid's dress I bought for my stepsister Olivia's wedding, the Barbie pink one with the gigantic bow across my butt. She uninvited me when Candace found out I was in the wedding party, but the dress couldn't be returned.

Now that I'm done with teaching, I live in a handful of jeans and yoga pants, with equally casual tops. I consider pulling on a stretched-out pair of leggings and knotting a T-shirt at my waist, but I don't have the swagger—or the rail-thin body—to pull that off.

The answer, of course, lurks in the back of my closet, on the very last hanger. I pull out the dress I bought for Jason's proposal, the one I wore the night he broke up with me.

Why not?

It's not like I'm going to see anyone I know.

I dig out my fancy bra and panties, rescuing them from the very back of my dresser drawer. They fit like a dream, and I remember all over again why I spent a month's food budget on them.

Shimmying into my dress, I suck in my breath so I can wrestle the hidden side zipper into place. On my first try, it catches an inch shy of the top, and I have to twist like a seal to ease it back down.

Forget about a fairy godmother. I need a flock of happy bluebirds to get me properly dressed.

I glance back at the fire escape, but Gorgeous and his friends haven't returned. That's okay—I can't imagine how many peanuts it would take to train them to be my personal maids. I close the window and nudge the lock into place.

The zipper slides home on my second try. Barefoot, I pad into the bathroom where I have to hunt for the crimson lipstick I bought for my non-existent proposal. I finally find it, behind an empty bottle of Leo's body wash.

Forget about Leo. Seriously. For just one night.

Lips shiny and red, I tackle my hair. It's too heavy to stay in any up-do. I brush it until it shines and leave it down around my shoulders.

My shoes wait in the back of my closet, narrow stilettos with sky-high heels. My ankles are strong. I've spent the past five years walking two miles a day to campus, and two miles back.

Good thing, too, because my fancy carriage has gone the way of my fairy godmother and my bluebird attendants. I find the tiny clutch purse I bought for Proposal Night, and I drop in my phone, my apartment key, and the scratched keycard I'll need for the front door.

My last stop before I leave the apartment is the kitchen. I know better than to drink on an empty stomach. I open the cupboard, but the offerings are slim—a couple of Cup O'

Noodles and a blue box of macaroni and cheese that I won't take time to cook. The refrigerator isn't much better—some limp carrots, a carton that used to be leftover beef with broccoli, and an apple.

But I find a hunk of cheddar cheese at the back of the deli drawer. Miraculously, it hasn't begun to sprout green mold. I cut thick slices and eat them with the apple. Something's better than nothing.

Okay. Time to go. I have to be back by midnight—any later, and I'll be locked out of the apartment for good. I'll pack my meager belongings in the morning.

Out on the street, I make a quick detour to withdraw cash from the ATM—ten crisp twenty-dollar bills. I fold them carefully and tuck them into my clutch.

I've already chosen where I'm going. It's an underground bar, literally below ground level, a few blocks from campus. It's called Debasement, which made me laugh the first time I saw it, but made Jason scowl. I've seen people go down the steps there. They seem happy. They seem fun.

I walk through the muggy evening, wondering if people are looking at me, worrying that they know. *That woman is being evicted.*

She doesn't have a single friend to call, not even family.

All she has is a brother who lied to her. Again.

I grit my teeth and run my fingers through my hair. No one is looking at me. No one cares.

Forget. About. Leo.

I'm a block away from Debasement when I see the flashing lights—red and blue bouncing off the plate-glass storefronts. As I reach the bar, I realize a pair of patrol cars is parked directly in front.

Two policemen are wrestling a man up the concrete stairs that lead to the underground bar. He's twisting like a strung-up catfish, his hair sticking out all over, his face the color of plums. His hands are cuffed behind his back.

"You'll pay for this!" he shouts down the steps. "Your ass is mine!"

The police pause as they reach ground level, adjusting their grips on the man, who truly looks—and sounds—deranged. The criminal jackknifes, stretching his neck to hawk a huge gob of spit down the stairs.

"That's for you, asshole!" he shouts. "Think you're a big man? Getting the cops to do your dirty work? Fuck you! I'm gonna kill you!"

The closest policeman yanks hard enough that I hear the screaming man's teeth snap shut. "Hey, scumbag! That's assault, on top of everything else." The cop looks down the stairs. "Do you want to press charges, sir?"

"No thank you, officer."

That voice is as smooth as melted copper, warm and fluid in the evening breeze. It washes over me like a physical thing, stroking my spine from the nape of my neck to my tailbone.

I gape as a man tops the stairs, a perfect man, a man with the ideal body to match that molten voice. He's taller than either cop or the squirming guy in custody. He's broad, too—his shoulders stretch the seams of his sleek black T. His black jeans fit like they were sewn just for him.

Green eyes flash beneath spiky chestnut hair, and he steps too close to the man between the cops. A tiny white rectangle slips between his fingers, and I realize he's holding a business card.

"You're going to kill me, motherfucker?" he says, and now his flowing copper voice is forged into a sharp-edged spear. He shoves his card into the other man's breast pocket. "My name's Prince. Travis Prince. And you can find me at Diamond Freeport—if you fucking dare."

4

TRAP

~

I TALK BIG, BUT THE LOOGIE ON THE STEPS BEHIND ME WOKE THE fucking Beast inside my head.

My pulse is racing. My palms are slick with sweat. My lungs need more air, and pain clamps my skull like a charley horse, but I refuse to pant like a goddamn dog.

Instead, I clench both hands into fists, squeezing until my knuckles bulge like stone.

Once.

Twice.

Three times.

Four.

Five.

The Beast retreats.

The fucking nightmare fizzes into a rage that makes me want to break the asswipe's face. But the cops are loading him into one of the black-and-whites. Going after him now will only punch my own ticket to the station. If I land in a holding cell with that cocksucker, I'll end up facing a murder beef.

I narrow my eyes as the car door slams. The asshole throws himself against the window, screaming something I can't hear. I shoot him both middle fingers, waiting until the car takes the corner to drop my fists.

It's time to tighten security around the freeport. That shit-for-brains won't make it past the front gate, but we need to bring the biometrics online anyway.

I turn back to the bar, steeling myself to get past the mess on the steps. Beast or no Beast, I have a fresh-poured shot of WhistlePig waiting downstairs.

That's when I see her—a woman standing on the sidewalk.

She's staring at me like I'm Christmas, Easter and her fucking birthday all tied up in a bow. Her made-up face is pretty, but she's trying too hard, like she found that lipstick in her mother's bathroom drawer.

This is not a girl who spends a lot of time in bars, watching dirtbags get dragged out by Dover's finest.

Some part of my lizard brain kicks me in the balls, and I force myself not to stare at her tits. Instead, I start looking at her legs and the invitation of her fuck-me shoes, which I'm only too happy to oblige.

So I miss the expression on her face when she says, "Let me guess. He left a lousy tip?"

That catches me by surprise and I laugh, even though adrenaline still smokes the back of my throat. "Fucker waited for one of the college girls to go to the john and then he tried to roofie her drink."

"Tried?"

I flex my fingers. My knuckles are bruised, but the skin isn't split. "I got in his way."

"My hero," she says.

And the funny thing is, I feel like a good guy when she says it.

I want this little princess. She's exactly what I need. After all, I'm celebrating. Five years of legal hell, and I finally got government clearance to run Diamond Freeport as a tax haven.

Not one of the girls downstairs looks old enough to drink, much less consent to my twisted demands. But this little number, in her painted-on dress… Those red, red lips are killing me. But the thing that really shoots steel into my cock is the sense that she hasn't played this game before.

I can't say how I know. It's nothing she does, nothing she says. Hell, I don't think she's *said* a dozen words.

But I'm suddenly certain she's the reason I came to Debasement tonight. We'll have a drink together. Maybe two.

And then I'll fuck her on my terms—bound, gagged, and gone by dawn.

5

ALIX

~

I SHOULD BE SCARED OF THIS GUY.

He towers over me, even though I'm wearing heels. When he flexes his fingers, I see his knuckles are red. He *punched* the guy the cops took away.

But he did it to protect a woman. He took a risk for a stranger. So I say, "Your name's Prince? Like Prince Charming?"

"More like the Prince of Darkness."

His slow smile kindles a Fourth of July sparkler deep inside my belly. No. Not my belly. *Down there.*

Not breaking my gaze, he edges back, clearing a path for me to approach the steps. "You were heading to Debasement?"

The copper's back in his voice, warm and fluid, like honey glinting in the sun. I catch the wry twist of his lips, the insinuation in his tone. I smile past my nerves and say, "I should take the fifth on that."

"Take whatever you want. That's what I do."

He's not talking about corny legal terms. The sparkler settles into a steady flame, low and slow. My body loves his sly words, even as my mind says I should slow things down.

But I don't have time to go slow. I need to be home by midnight. I've only got this little pocket of time, this magical space where nothing matters, where nothing is real. Six hours of freedom, before I turn back into a responsible, care-burdened woman.

That's when I decide to change my name—just for tonight. Here, at Debasement, I won't be Alix. Tonight, I'm…Ella.

Ella is fun. Ella is light. She knows how to make a man—how to make Travis Prince—look at her with hunger in his eyes.

"Can I buy you a drink?" he asks.

Alix has never dreamed of accepting a drink from a stranger. But Ella knows exactly what to do. She smirks and says, "Just one?"

"You think you can handle more?"

He's not talking about alcohol. I almost lose my nerve and tell him I made a mistake. I need to go home. But he gestures for me to precede him down the stairs, and that's exactly what Ella wants.

Ella wants his eyes on her butt.

That's nasty and wrong and I've never wanted a stranger to ogle me before. But when I walk past Travis Prince, I expect to feel his palm brush the small of my back. And when he doesn't touch me, I'm actually disappointed.

The air-conditioned bar feels icy after the summer heat outside, and I blink hard to help my eyes adjust to the dark. Everyone applauds as Travis steps in behind me. I turn to catch the mountainous roll of his shoulders under his tight black T. He's uncomfortable with the attention.

The redhead behind the bar waves him over. "Your money's no good tonight," she says.

"Not necessary, Caitlyn," he says.

She ignores him with a saucy smile, selecting a bottle from

the mirrored wall behind her. I admire her easy grace, the way she teases, striking a pose with the liquor. "Your first glass didn't make it through the war. Still want the Pig?"

He nods and she gives him a generous pour over a single baseball-size sphere of ice. He inclines his head toward me and says, "And my friend will have..."

Ordinarily, I'd say a lemon drop, or maybe a cosmo, something sweet and fruity. But as Travis's hand closes around his rye, I want something simpler. Something more mature. "Grey Goose," I say. "On the rocks."

Caitlyn smiles like I've made the best choice in the world but before she reaches for a bottle, she says, "I'll have to see some ID."

"Sure, um, of course." I find my driver's license in my clutch and hand it over.

"Oh!" Caitlyn says. "Happy birthday!"

I blush, even though I haven't done anything weird. As Caitlyn pours my drink, Travis slides a hundred-dollar bill from his wallet and shoves it deep inside the beer mug holding tips.

Who is this guy? A crime-fighting millionaire superhero? I bet he rescues stray kittens from trees and helps little old ladies cross the street.

But the look he gave me outside, at the top of the stairs, told me loud and clear he wasn't any Boy Scout. I wonder what it would take for him to give *me* a hundred-dollar tip.

I can't believe I just thought that.

"Trap!" Caitlyn says, digging out the bill and trying to hand it back to him.

"What happened to 'the customer's always right?'" he asks. He flashes her a smile that is somehow friendly and feral at the same time. I want him to look at me the exact same way.

She holds up her hands in resignation. "Okay, okay. You win."

"I always do," he says levelly.

He salutes her with his glass before returning his attention to me. I've never met anyone like him before, with his brash confidence and his absolute certainty. Here in the bar, his eyes are the almost-black of forest underbrush, and I look down, needing to escape their intensity.

My fancy lace bra is doing nothing to keep my nipples from straining against my dress. I try to tell myself I'm reacting to the chill in the air, but that's Alix's lie. Ella knows the truth.

"Join me?" Travis—Trap?—asks, gesturing toward a booth in the back.

I shouldn't. I don't know this man. I shouldn't follow him into a dark corner.

Ella says yes.

Crossing in front of the bar, we pass a woman who's crying at a table for four, a sweating glass of ice water at her elbow. A friend is comforting her, saying, "It wasn't your fault. He was a creep. You had no way of knowing."

The crying woman must be the one whose drink was almost doctored. I'm still looking over my shoulder as I approach the booth Trap indicated, and I stumble over the step up to the private alcove.

Before I can lose even a drop of my icy vodka, Trap's hand closes over my elbow. The hungry thing inside me presses hard *down there*, making me gasp a little. "Thanks," I say, trying to catch my breath.

He doesn't answer. Instead, he takes a seat opposite me, setting his glass on the table with a precise thud. He spreads his right hand, the one that just rescued me from sprawling on Debasement's floor. He taps his thumb against the table, then moves each finger in turn—index, middle, ring, pinky—like he's playing scales on an invisible piano.

After he finishes, the silence stretches between us, lumpy and awkward. So I say, "Trap? Not Travis? Trap sounds like something to avoid."

He shrugs with one shoulder. "My father's name was Travis too. 'Trap' kept things simple."

"Then you're not as dangerous as you seem?"

"I wouldn't say that," he growls.

The thing inside me rolls over and I realize, once again, that I was wrong about his eyes. They're jungle eyes—green and gold and wild.

Before I can answer his declaration—is there *any* way to answer that?—the college women from the four-top approach. "Excuse me," says the one who was crying.

Trap looks at her calmly.

"I just wanted to say, like, thank you. I *know* I shouldn't have left my drink there. I mean, they told us that in *Freshman* Week. But I never thought anyone would do something *here*. It's like, *Dover*, you know? We're supposed to be *safe*. We're, like, not even a *mile* off campus. I mean, who would expect a creep like *that* in Dover?"

Her friend elbows her, a tight little gesture that finally puts the brakes on the runaway train of words.

The woman Trap rescued swallows hard, then raises her chin. She offers Trap her hand, like she's sealing a job interview. "Thank you," she says, her tone grave.

"Take care of yourself," Trap says, nodding curtly. But her hand still hangs there, fingers trembling just a little. He sets his jaw and shakes, his palm engulfing hers. I wonder what his heavy fingers would feel like, surrounding mine like that.

The two women scurry away. Trap puts his right hand back on the table and plays his imaginary musical scale—thumb, index, middle, ring, pinky.

His scowl makes Alix think about following those two freshmen out of the bar. But Ella raises her glass and takes a delicate sip.

The vodka is snowmelt off a glacier, so cold it glides down my throat without a hint of alcoholic burn. It settles in my belly like a crystal star of courage and I drink again, a healthier swallow this time.

Trap curls his fingers into a fist, like he's barely resisting the urge to play more notes. He doses himself with a healthy gulp of rye.

I've got five years of graduate level psychology courses under my figurative belt. I know not to throw around words like obsessive-compulsive disorder—OCD—but I recognize a tic when I see one.

He needed to ground himself after he saved me from falling. And again, after shaking hands with his damsel in distress. Touch is his trigger. Touching someone makes him seek escape.

I look up from his fisted hand, and those jungle eyes are waiting for me. "Wh—" I start and have to clear my throat. "Where were we?"

"You were making the mistake of thinking I'm not dangerous. I was correcting you."

Correction. Something in Ella—in me—wants to test him. Wants to see what will happen if I make another mistake. Wants to know exactly how far he'll go in *correcting* me.

Before I can act on such a crazy thought, I grab for my vodka, barely taking time to match my lips to the scarlet print on the glass's rim.

"You have an advantage here," he says. When he watches me swallow, it feels like he can see through my dress, past the lace of my bra, all the way to my flushed and feverish skin. I don't feel like I have any advantage here. I don't have any control at all.

His teeth flash white as he says, "You know my name, but I don't know yours."

"Ella," I say, cementing my lie by finishing my drink with a gulp. I make up a last name. "Ella Locke."

"Would you like another drink, Ella?" he asks.

I shouldn't. The roof of my mouth is already buzzing. I'm much too interested in the curve of Trap's lips, in his shark-like smile as he waits for my response.

But *no* is off the table till midnight. So I square my shoulders and say, "Yes, please."

He raises a hand and gets Caitlyn's attention. We talk while we wait, about the weather maybe, or how the Phillies are doing, or recent studies in how the perihypoglossal nuclei function as part of the brain's complex circuitry related to eye movements.

Something like that. The humming in my ears distracts me.

By the time the bartender finally brings my drink, I'm digging deep for a fresh topic of conversation. "Diamond Freeport," I say, folding my hands around my new glass. "You told the jerk that's where you work?"

"Not exactly," Trap says. "I *own* Diamond Freeport."

It sounds like something in *Star Wars*, a place where spaceships dock to trade goods with aliens. So I ask, "And that is... what, exactly?"

There's that one-shouldered shrug again. "Basically, it's a warehouse."

"What's the not 'basic' part?"

His smile strokes me like I'm a cat. The thing *down there* wants to arch toward him, to twist and curl to get closer to his touch. "We have a special tax status. As of midnight tonight, deals inside Diamond are tax-free. That's why I'm here. I'm celebrating."

"Wait!" I say. "I'm celebrating too!"

"Imagine that," he drawls. And the wild thing in his eyes dances with the yearning thing inside me. I have to press my thighs together to keep from trembling *down there*. And try as I might, I can't think of a single thing to say.

6

TRAP

I'M BORED BY THE BULLSHIT.

I want to lean across the table and plant my thumb on her bottom lip. I want to tell her, "Look, little girl. You're begging to be fucked, with your big-girl makeup and your painted-on dress and your sky-high heels. And I *need* to fuck—that's the whole reason I'm here. So we both know it's gonna happen and we can forget all about polite conversation and just have another drink."

Point of pride, though: I've never forced a woman. And there's no way a drunk woman can consent to the things I plan to do tonight.

But I'm not opposed to stacking the deck a little in my favor.

If I can get her to the freeport, if she sees my house, sees the way I live, she'll be more inclined to accept the way I need to fuck her. Even if—*especially* if—I give her a chance to sober up once she's there. I just need to get her loose enough to take that first step, to come home with me.

So, it's back to the bullshit.

"If I'm a billionaire…" she says. The phrase must strike her as funny because she cuts herself short to laugh.

"If you're a billionaire…" I salute her with my glass, like she's on to something special. She answers with another gulp of Grey Goose.

Good girl. She's a very good girl. I shift on the booth's upholstered bench, easing the pressure of my jeans against my cock.

Ella polishes off the last of her second vodka and sets the glass on the table with a decisive clink. She frowns. "Impossible. I'll never be a billionaire."

"Never say never."

She shakes her head with a vehemence that tells me it's time. She's ready. "Not gonna happen."

I give her my best good-guy shrug. "That doesn't mean you can't see the freeport."

She pins me with a shrewd look. She's not as far gone as I thought she was. "What d'you mean?"

"Come home with me. Let me give you a personal tour of Diamond. I've got paintings and jewelry and luxury cars…"

She laughs, sitting back in the booth. "Do a lot of women fall for that?"

It was a long shot. But I match her laugh and say, "Come on. I'm celebrating. You're celebrating. Let's celebrate together."

Too much, too fast. She frowns. "My mother told me never to get in a car with a stranger."

I think about asking what her mother would say about how her tits are falling out of her dress, but I don't think that'll get her any closer to gagging on my cock. So instead I say, "Then ask me a question. I'll tell you whatever you want to know, and we won't be strangers anymore."

She tilts her head, considering. "I can ask anything?"

I spread my hands wide. "I've got nothing to hide."

"What's the deal with your counting to five?"

Every sip of rye I've had turns to a separate brick of ice in my belly. The Beast roars its evil laugh. "Five?" I ask, pretending to be confused.

"When you touched me. When you shook hands with that student. Why'd you have to play five notes after that?"

The Beast snarls as my fingers fold into fists.

There are plenty of other women in Dover. Some of them will come to Debasement tonight. I can chain one of *them* to my bed.

I don't want some other woman. I want Ella. I want her wide wicked mouth and her thick dark hair and her timid, tempting body.

But the price will be telling her the truth.

Or part of the truth, anyway.

I take a deep breath and exhale slowly. "I saw something when I was a kid. Had to touch it. When I think about it now, I need to move to make the memory go away."

It's the first time I've ever said the words out loud. The first time I've told a soul.

She's quiet for so long I think I've lost her. I've said too much. I'm too fucked up—and she doesn't even know what I'm going to do to her back at the freeport.

So I steel myself and take her hand. I fold my fingers around hers deliberately. I feel her warmth against mine, the softness of her skin, the pulse at the base of her thumb.

The Beast howls, but I wait for Ella to meet my gaze, to acknowledge that I did this just for her. Finally, she nods, a tiny dip of her chin.

I swallow and say, "Come home with me, Ella. Nothing will happen that you don't want. I promise."

7

ALIX

I can't believe I'm actually considering Trap's offer.

Wait. That's a lie. I'm not considering. I've already made up my mind.

I just have to figure out how to protect myself.

I think about the college woman, the one who nearly had her drink roofied. She wasn't safe, even with her friend here at the bar.

I don't have any friends. All I have is Leo.

It feels foolish to trust my safety to my brother. He's already proven he can't be relied on.

But there's a big difference between earning a dark blue chip at NA and keeping his sister safe. Leo may be back at square one with his recovery, but he can still be my back-up on this. He'll be there for me if I really, truly need him. If it's life or death.

I take out my phone and say to Trap, "I'm telling my brother where I'm going."

"Good idea," he says.

I tap the screen. "I'm sending him your name."

"Smart."

"And the name of Diamond Freeport."

"Excellent."

"What's the address? Where're you taking me?"

I feel the weight of Trap's jungle gaze as I type in the destination. He gives me the zip code too, even the plus-four. I stare at the screen after I send the last line, waiting, hoping, praying that Leo writes back.

Nothing. No three dots. No response at all.

"Anything else?" Trap asks. "Anyone else you want to tell?"

I don't want him to know the truth. I don't want to say I'm alone in the world. I put my phone back in the clutch. "Nope. I'm good."

He nods and climbs to his feet, making a sweeping gesture toward Debasement's front door. I walk in front of him, hyper-aware of how my hips sway as I plant my feet, courtesy of my high-heel shoes.

As I walk by the bar, Caitlyn is polishing a glass with a white towel. "Have a good night," I say, purposely drawing her attention.

She gives me a knowing smile. "You too."

I wonder if she's walked the same path I'm taking right now. Has Trap invited her back to Diamond Freeport? Is that the reason they're on a first-name basis? Do I care?

If I'm honest, the idea bothers me.

But I have zero right to make that claim. Alix is a woman who dreams of dedicated boyfriends, of committed relationships. But I'm Ella tonight. And Ella doesn't care.

I lead the way up the stairs to street level. Another man might take my hand as we move down the sidewalk, might even pull me close to his side. But I already know Trap won't do that.

Which makes me wonder: If brushing my hand was enough to trigger a traumatic compulsive response, how can Trap possibly expect to make love? Because I have no delusions—he absolutely intends to take me to bed.

I consider asking him, right then and there. But this is my night of saying *yes*. Whatever answer he gives, I'm not changing my mind. I've made that promise to myself.

Am I actually brave, or are the two shots of Grey Goose doing the talking? I set my jaw. What difference does it make? The result is the same.

I'm going to Diamond Freeport with Trap Prince.

I follow him down a narrow alley, between the building that houses Debasement and the boutique clothing store next door. I cross the tiny parking lot, weaving between cars. My ankle starts to turn on the uneven surface, but I steady myself against a gray Camry.

So I'm barely paying attention when Trap stops beside the most beautiful car I've ever seen. It's a dark shimmering blue, as if the paint is lit from deep inside. Its body is low to the ground, sculpted with the grace of a hunting panther. Everything about the car says power and speed, masterful control of the road. Of the world.

I realize Trap has opened the passenger door. He's waiting for me to move forward, to finalize his invitation.

I wish I'd insisted on a third drink. I wish I had more courage.

Forcing a laugh, I ask, "Who'd you sell your soul to, for this?"

His answer is pitched low, just for me. "Who says I ever had a soul?"

The car is very beautiful. The seat is very low. Trap shifts his weight. He extends a hand, beckoning, welcoming.

Yes. This is the night for *yes*.

With my left hand, I twitch my dress higher, raising its hem to the middle of my thighs. With my right hand, I steady myself, using Trap's outstretched fingers as my anchor.

He trembles when I touch him, but his hand closes over mine. Strong. Steady. Stable.

He waits until I'm settled before he closes my door. If he needs to tap through his five-point ritual, he does it before he slides into the driver's seat.

The engine roars to life—fierce and bold instead of the tamed purr I expect. I wonder if this is how Cinderella felt, settling in her crystal carriage with a matched team of horses and a uniformed footman attending to her every need.

Cinderella's ride was just a pumpkin, I remind myself. She stayed out past midnight and nearly ruined everything. I don't have that luxury. Not tonight. Not if I want to maintain the few possessions I still own.

I glance at the dashboard, at the smooth, orderly gauges. A clock displays the time: 6:27. Five and half hours left of *yes*. Trap shifts gears, and the needy thing inside me shifts as well, flooding *down there* with warmth.

Maybe I'm supposed to make small talk. Tell jokes. Say something about Trap's muscled forearm as his fingers caress the gearshift.

But I'm afraid I'll break the spell if I talk. I'll lose my nerve. I'll forget about *yes* and tumble back to *no, no, no*.

We pass the Sherman campus. We reach the edge of town. We leave behind Wal-Mart and Home Depot. Orderly rows of corn march beside the road.

If Trap is nervous, he doesn't give any sign. His hands are steady on the wheel, not a tremor in sight. He scans the road before us with casual competence.

I concentrate on breathing.

We've been in the car fifteen minutes when Trap turns into a private driveway. Trees arch over us as we approach an iron gate.

He brakes to a stop and lowers his window. Reaching toward a metal box, he types in a combination. It looks long, eight or nine digits at least. After a moment's hesitation, the gate glides open.

Glancing over my shoulder, I see a towering brick wall on either side of the gate. An iron cage is built into the wall, the type of one-way revolving door that guards inner-city subway stations, letting riders exit while keeping fare jumpers from breaking in. Concertina wire curls on top, metal teeth glinting in the evening sun.

Trap pulls into a paved courtyard. A construction site spreads to our left, a gaping hole ringed by wooden fences and guarded by a pair of bulldozers. Directly in front of us stands a six-story glass and chrome office building complete with another security box.

But Trap guides the car to the right.

A neatly trimmed lawn sets off a two-story building. It's made of white brick, I think, or maybe perfectly stacked stone. The walls are stark, sharp with precise right angles. About one third of the way from the driveway, there's an alcove, a diagonal slash that might lead to a door. There's not a window in sight.

Trap guides the car to the right, around the side of the shimmering white building. A garage waits for us, dark and spare. Trap parks in the middle of the open space, taming the engine with the quick tap of a button.

I could wait for him to circle the car, to open my door and hand me out like I'm a princess, but I'm perfectly capable of exiting on my own. I shut the door carefully, maybe more gently than it requires.

I can't imagine living in a pile of stone—cold and bleak, not a single sign of life. What happened to Trap when he was a child? What—or who—was he forced to touch? What broke this man, and how did he put himself back together inside this silent castle?

Trap moves to a featureless door. He types another passcode into a panel, pausing long enough for some inner electronics to work. The door sweeps open.

I need to move. I need to walk. But once I cross that threshold, will I remember how to shape my lips around tonight's word—*yes?*

The jungle is back in Trap's eyes. He takes in the rucked line of my skirt, the twist of fabric exposing my right thigh and the edge of my black lace panties. His gaze pokes the creature inside me, sending another hopeful shiver *down there*.

He steps back to let me enter before him. I'm still feeling Caitlyn's vodka, so I settle my palm against the door frame as I step inside the house. And I almost collapse against Trap's broad chest behind me.

I'm standing in a kitchen, but it's like no kitchen I've ever seen before. There's a granite island large enough to land a 747, with a spotless steel sink bigger than the bathtub in my dingy apartment. There's a pair of ovens, in case anyone needs to roast a couple of buffalo, and an induction cooktop the size of a soccer field. I don't see a refrigerator, but I bet one or two are hidden in the wall of honey-colored wood that stretches from floor to ceiling to my left.

But none of that is the most amazing thing about the kitchen. The most amazing thing about the kitchen is the curved wall of glass that swoops around a courtyard, a hidden oasis invisible from the driveway at the front of the house. I'm drawn to the windows like a swallow flying home.

The wall of glass continues beyond the kitchen. The entire back of the house is clear, a swaying organic shape. On the ground floor, I can glimpse a book-lined library and an austere office, computer screens erected in a forbidding fence. A living room offers leather couches and sleek chairs, arranged around a thick white rug that makes my toes curl inside my shoes. A dining room table is large enough for twelve.

I can't see the rooms directly above us, but a bedroom waits on the upper floor, directly across from the kitchen. A stern black comforter stretches over a Montana-size bed, corners made crisp against matching iron headboard and footboard.

Swallowing hard, I turn to see Trap watching me. His fingers curl easily by his sides. He carries his weight on the balls of his feet, like he's ready to spring, to catch me if I stumble or to drag me to his lair.

There isn't enough air in the kitchen. My knees tremble, and for the first time that day, my ankles forget how to support me in my shoes. I wonder what I'm doing here. Whether *yes* is really right for me.

I want to ask him for a shot of vodka, a booster for the drinks I had at Debasement. I want to tell him I need a minute; my brain has to catch up with my body. I want to say I'm overwhelmed, that I thought I could do this but maybe I was wrong, and I might want to go home.

He steps toward me and my breath catches, freezing somewhere deep inside my chest. I close my eyes, but I can still feel the drinks Caitlyn poured for me, and the floor rolls beneath my feet. I open my eyes and steady myself with a palm on the kitchen island's endless plain of granite.

Yes, I remind myself.

Yes, I want this.

Yes, I need this.

"All right," Trap says, and his voice sounds different now. There's a snap of command, a hidden core of iron that makes me wonder if I imagined the honey-melt of copper outside Debasement. "First things first."

I brace myself. This is it. This is why I'm here. This is what I chose.

"You," Trap says, and every muscle in my body tenses. "You need a glass of water."

8

TRAP

~

THE LOOK OF RELIEF ON ELLA'S FACE IS SO TRANSPARENT THAT something hitches inside my chest. I almost regret that she's the one I brought here.

Almost.

But she's here and she's mine and my cock is tired of waiting. She needs to sober up so I can fuck her blind.

Two drinks. Two hours. And it's already been thirty minutes since she took her last sip at Debasement. Plus, I don't need her stone, cold sober. Just clear-headed enough to make an honest choice.

Call it an hour of waiting. 7:40.

"Make yourself at home," I say, and my smile is real. She takes one of the bar stools, like she's not certain how much longer she can stand.

I want to know if her knees are shaking. I want to make her thighs tremble. I want to feel the slick of her pussy against the palm of my hand as she grinds her clit against my wrist.

I want a thousand things I'll never have, even if she stays after I tell her everything she'll have to do.

"Water?" I ask, like I'm not picturing her spread-eagled on my bed.

Her eyes shoot to mine, and I read an entire novel there. She wants another shot of vodka. She wants to numb herself, to take herself away. I can't figure out what brought her out tonight, why she's wearing that fucking dress, why she chose those shoes. But whatever demons she's fighting, she wants a security blanket, a barrier between her desire and mine.

Too bad that's the last thing I intend to give her.

Finally, she nods. I open the fridge and pull out a bottle of Berg. I crack the cap and put it on the island in front of her.

"Ice?" I ask, retrieving a glass from one of the hidden cupboards.

She nods again, and I slide open the unseen icemaker. The cubes are clear as air and cold as my scarred heart. I fill her glass to the rim.

"Hungry?"

Her eyes are wide, and if I hadn't been with her every second of the past hour, I'd wonder if she was riding some sort of chemical high. But her chin dips again, so I open the disguised fridge.

I'm glad she wants to eat. I want to feed her. I wish I could give her bread and cheese and a bottomless bowl of rice to soak up the alcohol in her blood, but those are frat-boy tricks that don't really work. The only thing that will get her sober is time.

I pull out a basket of strawberries. For just a moment, I imagine crushing them against her skin, starting with her lips and moving down her throat to her tits, to the high tight nips I caught a glimpse of when she first walked into Debasement.

The Beast growls. That's another thing I'll never get to do— rub fresh juice into her, skin against skin. At least I can watch her eat, hear her breath catch as the first bright taste of a berry explodes across her tongue.

I won't imagine anything else exploding across her tongue.

Not now.

Not yet.

"So…" she finally says, and I wonder what *she's* been thinking while I've been imagining the sounds she'll make when she comes for the fifth time.

"So," I answer, tossing back the conversational ball. I press my hands against the granite island. I'm a twenty-nine-year-old captain of modern industry, not a hard-dicked high-school geek.

I can't remember the last time a woman got to me this way.

Who the fuck am I kidding? No woman has ever gotten to me this way.

She drains her glass, letting the ice cubes nudge the soft spot between her lips and nose. Without my prompting, she pours herself more water. I resist the urge to glance at the clock set into the cooktop's control panel. I promised her an hour.

I'm a sick, twisted bastard, but I'm a man of my word.

"*So*," she says with a little more force. "This freeport of yours. There are other ones, right? Your competition?"

Jesus fucking Christ. Are we back to talking about business? But maybe that'll make my cock stand down.

"A handful right now. More should open in the next few years."

"Why would anyone work with you?"

I consider being offended, but it's a good question. "My environmental controls were designed by the top experts in the world. Temperature in the fine arts galleries will fluctuate less than one one hundredth of a degree."

"Okay…" She doesn't sound convinced.

"The construction out there," I say, nodding in the general direction of the plaza. "It'll have state-of-the-art conference rooms." That sounds even more boring than HVAC, so I quickly rattle off key facts and figures—my communication systems and recording facilities and top-of-the-line catering.

"All right," she says, clearly unimpressed.

"But?" I prod.

"Can't billionaires hire their own chefs? What makes Diamond Freeport special?"

"Sounds like you have something in mind."

"Diamond..." she says. "The hardest substance in the world. One of the rarest, right?"

She's stringing ideas together, adding up scraps of knowledge. If I can't fuck her yet, the next best thing is watching her think. "Right," I say.

"And one of the most valuable?"

I shrug. "Sure."

"So what's more rare, more valuable than time? No one— not even your billionaires—can make more of it. Invite your best customers to spend time together. Keep it exclusive. An even dozen."

I laugh. "Why would they do that?"

She ignores my challenge. "Call it...the Diamond Ring. Each month, invite the Diamond Ring to an exclusive event. Here. In your private home."

My refusal is automatic. Voice flat, I say, "I keep my private life separate from business."

She shakes her head like she knows me. Like she knows what I am. "Not anymore. Not if you want to make Diamond Freeport the most elite business venture in the world."

"What the *fuck* would I do with clients in this house?"

She's shocked by the *fuck*, but it only takes her a moment to shrug. "Throw a dinner party. Host a poker game. I don't know, give them pony rides and birthday cake and fireworks at midnight. The important thing is they're the only ones who ever set foot inside the door. They're the only ones who get that side of you. They're special. They're yours."

I poke the idea like a bruise. It's absurd, opening my home to *strangers*. That's why I built the office tower. That's why I'm investing in the conference center and new galleries.

But my clients won't be strangers once we've shared business strategies. Once we've invested our fortunes together. Once my millions direct their billions and the freeport yields profits beyond my wildest dreams.

My dreams are fucking wild.

I study Ella's face. She's more animated than she's been since she entered Debasement. Engaged. Confident. I say, "You seem pretty sure of yourself."

"I am." She doesn't seem to realize how her spine straightens with her simple declaration.

"Because…" I prompt.

"Because people love being part of an exclusive group. The more exclusive the better. It's simple psychology. The dorsolateral prefrontal cortex, ventrolateral prefrontal cortex, and anterior cingulate cortex mediate the modulation of emotion-elicited activation in limbic regions."

I stare.

"What?" she asks.

"I love it when you talk brainy to me."

She blushes. Her cheeks stain red like I've told her how much I want to bury my face in her snatch, eating her out until she loses her voice screaming my name.

As if the Beast would ever let me do that…

I can't help it. I look at the cooktop clock. 7:46.

Shit. I've wasted six minutes. Six minutes I could have spent…

I lean across the island and take away the berries. "It's time," I say.

She swallows hard, and she's back to being the girl I met at Debasement. Shy. Nervous. Determined. "Time?" she asks, and my cock twitches as the quiver in her voice.

"Time for me to tell you exactly what I'm going to do to you. And time for you to decide if you're going to stay."

9

ALIX

THIS MUST BE WHAT WHIPLASH FEELS LIKE.

One moment, I'm eating the sweetest fruit I've ever tasted in my life and sipping water that probably costs a hundred bucks a bottle. The next, I'm spouting psychology theory as if I'm in the middle of a graduate seminar.

And now I'm facing a man who looks like he's stripped me naked in his mind, like my sexy dress and my lacy underthings have melted away from the heat of his blazing eyes.

I'm scared.

But I'm excited, too, excited like I can't remember ever being before. Certainly I never felt like this in bed with Jason. Jason was a boy. This is the first time I've ever been with a man.

I lick my lips. I take a deep breath. I force myself to meet Trap's gaze, and I say, "Yes."

"Yes, what?"

"Yes. I'll do whatever you want."

He shakes his head. "That's not the way this works. You can't say that until you hear exactly what I'm going to do you. What you're going to do to me. With me. For me."

Every time he says "me" the thing *down there* pulses. I'm pretty sure my pretty silk panties are damp, which they've never been before.

He doesn't know tonight is my night of *yes*. But this is his house. His rules. And the first rule seems to be I have to listen and agree. "Okay," I say. "Tell me."

He plants his hands in front of him, spreading his fingers wide on the granite. I catch a flicker in his wrists, like he's fighting back the urge to play his imaginary scales.

"You'll walk upstairs to my bedroom," he says.

I nod.

"You'll take off all your clothes."

I nod.

"You'll enter my bathroom and turn on the shower, where you will wash exactly the way I order you to."

Order.

The word shoots through me. Alix wouldn't take orders from a stranger. She'd say *no* and leave.

But Ella likes the idea of being told what to do. She likes Trap being in charge. She trusts that he has a better imagination than she'll ever have.

I start to ask if he'll be watching me in the shower, but I already know the answer. I try to imagine what it will be like, if he'll order me to touch myself. If he'll make me wash *down there*.

Of course he will.

He's the victim of childhood trauma, apparently untreated. He's spent years developing workarounds to defuse the misfiring of his traumatized brain. This elaborate ritual is apparently how he functions sexually.

Plus, it sounds incredibly exciting.

I nod.

"Say it out loud. Tell me you'll follow my orders in the shower."

"I— I'll follow your orders in the shower."

He must have been afraid I'd say no because he exhales a huge breath. Then he comes to stand behind me. He leans in, his T-shirt pressing against the back of my dress, against my bare shoulders. He plants his arms beside mine, wide enough that we don't touch.

And he starts to whisper in my ear.

He tells me the rest of what he's going to do to me, every filthy word. My heart starts to race as I imagine giving up the control he demands. *No, no, no,* warns Alix.

Yes, sighs Ella.

I can feel the heat of his body. I can sense the wire strung through his limbs as, item by item, I consent.

"Yes, I'll follow your orders when you bind me."

"Yes, I'll follow your orders when you're gloved."

"Yes, I'll follow your orders…"

"Your orders…"

"Orders…"

Yes, yes, yes.

His voice is raw by the time he's finished. I'm shaking so hard he has to shift his arms, spread them wider to keep from touching me.

Everything he demands is sick. Perverted. Wrong. But Ella makes sure I say yes to every last command.

Finally, he grits: "And you'll be out of here by midnight."

"M—midnight?" I sound like I've never heard the word before. Somehow, I forgot my own limit on tonight. I forgot I need to be home before my keycard dies.

"No one sleeps over," Trap says, like it's some sort of punishment.

He's saving me from myself. "Yes," I say. "I'll be out of here by midnight."

Trap shudders at my final acceptance. I feel the ripple go

through his chest and down my spine. He pulls away, releasing the cage that's held me, and I embarrass myself by moaning when the cool kitchen air kisses the nape of my neck.

He smirks as he rounds the granite island. He waits until I raise my chin, until I meet his eyes.

"Are you a virgin, Ella?" he asks.

"Of course not!" I answer quickly, like that would be a terrible thing.

"Don't lie."

"I'm not lying!" And I'm not. Technically.

He waits for me to back down, but I don't. "I need to be sure," he says.

"If I were a virgin, would you send me home?"

"No," he answers slowly. "Not unless you ask to go. But if you're a virgin, I'll go more slowly. I'll do my best to keep from hurting you."

"I'm not a virgin," I confirm again. But I hear the warning, clearer than all the things I've already accepted. What Trap plans might hurt.

He nods, but I'm not sure he believes me. "We'll use a system," he says. "A code. If I ask you your color, green means you're fine. We can continue whatever we're doing. Yellow means you need more time. I'll slow down. Red is your safe-word. Red means stop. Immediately. With those rules in place, with those protections, will you stay with me until midnight?"

Yes. This is the night of *yes.*

"I'll stay," I say.

"Good girl."

I should bristle. I should fight. I'm not a girl; I'm a strong and independent woman.

But I think about the long nights since Jason walked out on me. I think about how I've touched myself. I think about all the books I've read and movies I've watched and how easy it's supposed to be to induce a sexual climax.

My brain knows Trap's proposal is a heart-stopping minefield. But my body wants to try. It wants to follow Trap's rules, his commands. It thinks this controlling man might be the only person in the universe who can make it work the way it's supposed to.

"My good, good girl," Trap says, and the flutter *down there* is so strong I have to clutch the counter.

10

TRAP

Sweet holy fuck.

She'll do it.

She's not the first, of course. In the past year, four other women have listened to my rules and been brave enough to stay.

The blonde who brayed like a donkey.

The pharmaceutical rep with the mole behind her knee.

The marathon runner with thighs like steel.

The brunette who screamed for Daddy when she came.

I should remember their names, but they're nothing to me. Each of them was nothing the moment I called a car and got her out the gate.

But Ella is different. She's special.

I don't know her story, why she's dressed like a whore but acts like she's dedicated her pussy to God. Maybe that's what sparked, the moment I saw her at the top of the Debasement steps. She's innocent. Clean. Pure enough to sing the Beast to sleep.

She's smart, too. The smartest woman I've ever dragged back to Diamond. She's got a secret or two, just like me.

She's sad.

"Hey," she says. "I want to do this. I really do. But can I have a drink before we start?" Her laugh sounds a little crazy. "Just one, for courage."

I should tell her no. She should be stone-cold sober. She should have every last wit about her so her safeword's really safe.

Oh, fuck it. One goddamn drink.

"I don't have Grey Goose," I say. "How about Belvedere?"

A quick frown flicks across her face. I realize she doesn't recognize the brand name. I could tell her it's made from rye, that it's unfiltered and heavy on botanicals, floral with a citrus edge.

Or I could pour her a fucking drink.

I fetch two glasses from the cupboard. Ice cubes, three each. I pad into the dining room for the bottle, but I'm back before she thinks about following me.

I pour with a steady hand, like I'm measuring ingredients for a bomb. After I pass her a glass, I raise my own, swirling the clear liquor around the ice. Once. Twice. Three times. Four. Five.

Fuck. I haven't even touched her and the Beast is stepping in.

Ella follows my motion, flexing her own wrist like there's a right way and a wrong way, and she's determined to follow the rules. I salute her, just raising my glass between us, and she answers with her own.

Before I can sip, she tosses back her entire shot, downing it like it's medicine.

Medicine.

Belvedere is eighty proof, forty percent pure alcohol. If we were soldiers on a battlefield, we could use it to sterilize our wounds.

She sets her glass on the counter with a decisive clank, still shuddering from the vodka hitting the back of her throat. Her lips part, and the tip of her tongue emerges, soft and pink and ready to swipe clean the last film of Belvedere.

I surge forward and crush her mouth with mine.

Heat.

Soft, wet, heat.

She opens to me, offering up her timid tongue, and I savage her lips against her teeth. I need her, all of her. I need her pressure. I need her breath. I need her startled, muffled squeal that changes to a hum when I pull back enough to find her tongue with mine.

A normal man would fold his palm behind her head. He'd turn her to a better angle, softening his lips in an invitation for her to press her body against his. He'd use his other hand to trace her curves, to make her feel good, to gain her trust.

I'm not normal. I'm broken and jagged and barely holding on to what passes for sane.

I grip the metal back of the stool she's sitting on, clench it tight enough that my knuckles pop. I turn the chair, the whole chair, so I can deepen the kiss for both of us.

She stays with me. She tilts her head. She presses forward, breathing an urgent, wordless plea for more. Her hands move toward my shoulders, but she stops herself with a tiny gasp that I drink down with all the rest.

Fuck. I can't remember the last time I kissed a woman like this. Who am I kidding? I've *never* kissed a woman like this, not with this heat, not with this desperation, not with this bottomless, shattering need.

I want to devour her. I want to suck the breath out of her lungs. I want to drink the blood out of her veins. I want, I want, I want…

Gradually, my brain stirs back to life. I realize that I'm standing in my kitchen, hulking over a woman who's trapped between the iron back of a bar stool and a hard stone counter. I'm *kissing* a woman, mixing her spit with mine, breathing her breath with mine, exposing myself to everything she's brought into my house.

I soften my lips. I pull back. But before I lose her completely, before she pulls away, I catch her lower lip between my teeth. I feel its plump heat, its soft, wet weight, and I hear the moan that rises from her throat.

I bite her. My jaw tightens and my teeth close, hard enough to cause real pain. I tug, knowing it'll hurt her. I start to turn my head, to yank her lip between my clenched teeth, sharp enough to draw blood.

But I make myself step away.

Breathing like a stallion, I can't meet her eyes. I break my death-grip on the bar stool, loosening fingers that ache like they've been forced through the holes on a cheese grater. Flexing both hands, I force myself to grit out two damning syllables, "Color?"

She doesn't answer right away, and I know I'm a monster. I made a big show out of saying she'd have a choice, out of telling her every single way I was going to touch her, make her touch herself. And then I throw the entire fucking lie under the bus, jumping her like a rutting dog.

We had a deal, and I broke it. I lost the only thing I wanted before I even had a chance to see what it was.

"Wh—what?" she asks, her voice tiny and breathless and stunned. The back of her hand is pressed to her lip, and I realize I lost more control than I thought. She's bleeding.

"Color," I grit out. "Red? Yellow?"

"Green," she whispers. And then, as if she can't quite believe it herself, she says it again, full voice this time. "Green."

I see the question in her eyes. If I broke that rule, am I breaking all the others? Did I throw the entire playbook out with the booze?

For just a moment, I think about what that would be like. How it would feel to have a woman move under me any way she wanted. How her fingers would pull my hair as I ate her out, how her lips would close around my throbbing cock...

The Beast storms back like a Category 5 hurricane. Roaring, I pound the counter with my fist—once, twice, three times, four, five. I want to hurt myself. I want the bones in my hand to crack. I want to drive order back into my life. Power. Control.

When I can push words past the screaming monster in my brain, I repeat her single syllable. "Green."

She nods.

I swallow hard. "Then get your ass upstairs. In my shower. Now."

11

ALIX

I brush my lip with my fingertips as I climb the stairs to the second floor. It feels tender, bruised, and I want to never stop touching it.

I've never had a man kiss me like that before. Like he's dying. Like he's drowning. Like I'm the only thing keeping him from spinning out in space.

At the top of the stairs, I turn to the right, to the master bedroom I could see from the ground floor. My knees do something funny when I see the huge bed; they buckle, and I have to take a quick three steps forward to stay on my feet.

When I turn around, Trap fills the doorway. His arms are crossed over his broad chest, and his biceps pop in his tight black T. His feet are planted wide, like he's anchoring the world.

"Okay," he says. "Strip."

I look at the wall of windows. It's summer, so it's still light outside, but the sun is sinking into the thicket of trees at the far end of the sculpted lawn. No one can see inside. Yet. But the overhead lights are on a dimmer; the room is already filled with a golden glow. As twilight advances, Trap and I will be on display like actors in a play.

"You saw the gate," he says, as if I've spoken my fears out loud. "No one's getting back there. No one will see you but me." When I continue to hesitate, his voice cracks with command. "Ella! Strip!"

Alix is horrified. But Ella whispers *yes* as I work the side zipper on my dress. My fingers shake, triggered by equal parts of fear and anticipation. I've never done anything like this before. I've never *imagined* doing anything like this.

I wriggle out of my dress, letting it fall onto the thick white rug like a snake's shed skin.

The air in the room is cool, and my arms and legs immediately sprout goosebumps. They're not the only things reacting to the chill. The tips of my breasts harden so fast they hurt.

I catch my breath the same time Trap does. Part of me wants to close my eyes, to take myself away, to put miles and years between us.

But part of me wants to know what he's seeing. Part of me wants to know if I'm doing this right, if I'm being the woman he needs me to be.

His fingers tighten on his biceps as I twist for the back clasp on my bra. The two hooks break apart like he's bribed them. My breasts spill free as I slip the straps down my arms. I drop the bra on top of my dress.

"Shoes," Trap breathes.

I step out of the left stiletto, and then the right. The arches of my feet weep with relief as my bare soles settle onto the rug. I curl my toes, relishing my moment of freedom.

Trap's gaze strokes my legs, smoothing over my calves, my thighs. He settles hungrily on the scrap of lace around my hips. His intensity yanks the leash on the creature inside me, and I realize I'm more wet *down there* than I've ever been in my life.

He nods, and I slip my fingers beneath the edge of my

panties. The lace feels like it's printed on my skin. I pull the soft silk over my hips and let it slide to the floor. I take a single step forward, completely naked.

I want to cover myself. I want to spread my fingers across my breasts. I want to hide the soft curls *down there*.

But more than that, I want to see the wild light in Trap's eyes. I want him to be hungry. I want him to be mine.

Without waiting for his reminder, I skirt the bed. He's already told me what he needs next.

A wavy wall covered in tiny tiles separates the shower from the rest of the bathroom. As I round the bend, I see an array of four chrome controls. A rainfall shower head broader than my shoulders is suspended from the ceiling. Two jets are set in the wall, chest-high and waist-high. A hand-held spray snakes along beside them.

Remembering my instructions, I work the nearest control, waking the rainfall head. I set the temperature a notch short of scalding, just like Trap said I should. It seems like years have passed since he stood behind me in the kitchen.

It only takes a moment for steam to curl above the rainfall, a far cry from the ancient pipes I fight with every day at home. Trap has followed me; he's standing in the open doorway that leads out of this watery paradise. "Wash your hair," he prompts, his voice strangled.

Shampoo waits in a stone alcove, a sleek silver bottle from a brand I've never seen before. Conditioner stands beside it. My throat tightens when I see the other things on the shelf, but I ignore them for now.

I gasp when the scalding water hits my head. I start to reach for the control, to dial back the temperature, but I decide to give myself a moment, to see if I can adapt. After the initial shock, my body settles into the battering heat. My muscles soften like flame-licked candles, and a little of my nervousness swirls down the drain.

It's strange to wash my hair in front of someone else. The

shampoo smells like rosemary, sharp and clean and cooler than the water turning my skin pink. I'm conscious of my fingers massaging my scalp; I wonder what it would feel like to have Trap's hands in my hair.

I lather and rinse, repeating just the way it says on the bottle. The second time I work in the shampoo, it foams up in billowy clouds that cascade down my body. I finish by conditioning, finger-combing the rich cream from scalp to tips.

When I've rinsed again, my hair is as heavy and sleek as the pelt of some wild animal. Nearly languid, I look to Trap for my next instruction.

"Razor," he says, like the single word costs more than he can afford.

I knew this was coming. He told me downstairs: "And then you'll shave." I retrieve soap from the alcove, a creamy white bar that feels like it's made of buttermilk and dreams. A few turns between my palms builds a thick lather. I use my right hand to smooth suds over my left armpit.

The razor is heavy, fashioned from steel instead of the cheap plastic throw-aways I've used all my life. The head rotates like a precision surgical tool, and I glide it over the lather, slicing away the soap along with invisible stubble.

I make short work out of shaving under my right arm too. When I'm through, I return the razor to its shelf.

"Legs," Trap says.

Of course he wants my legs smooth. I should have realized that. I retrieve the soap and make more lather. It's awkward, bending down to work the razor around my ankle. I'm sure he's watching my bottom, but I can't make myself look up. I take my time, careful not to nick either knee.

When I finish, I look at Trap, eager for his nod of approval.

"Your bush," he says.

"Wh— what?"

"Shave your pubes."

I've never used that word in my life. I've certainly never

shaved my pubic hair. I know some women get waxed, and I've read about something called a Brazilian. But I've never even considered doing that to myself.

"Color," Trap snaps.

I could tell him red and leave forever. But the hibernating beast *down there* chooses that moment to turn over, sending a lazy, rolling ripple from my neck to my knees.

It doesn't want red.

It doesn't even want yellow.

"Green," I breathe.

"Trim first," he says. "Short." And I finally understand why the nail scissors are waiting on the shelf.

I grab a deep breath, pick up the scissors, and trim. Short.

When I finish, Trap tells me to use the shaving gel. "Stroke down with the razor. The direction the hair grows."

There's something about his tone—patient, calm—that makes me stare. He's asking me to do revolting things, but he's taking care of me at the same time. He's almost—I test the word in my mind and it fits—*kind.*

I shave carefully, rinsing the last of my hair down the drain. When I finish, I cup water against myself with my fingers, taking care to wash away the last of the shaving gel.

I gasp in surprise at the heat against skin that hasn't been bare since I was a child. Every nerve has been jolted awake. I run my fingernail over the surface and a tremendous shiver rolls from the crown of my head to my toes. Every muscle in my body tightens, and I laugh in wonder.

Trap, though, is nowhere near as amused.

"Wash everything," he commands. His voice is strained, barely evolved from a groan. I stop splashing water against my smooth, smooth skin and really take the time to look at him.

His hands are planted on his hips. His feet are locked hip-width apart. His jeans bulge at his zipper.

I've seen an aroused man before. I once asked Jason if it hurt. But judging from the line of Trap's jeans, his thing is huge.

My mind scrambles, and I try to remember everything he said he wants to do with it. A tremor of panic crawls across my belly.

"Start with your face," he says, like I haven't just been gaping at him. "End with your toes. Use the wall jets."

The instructions are exactly what I need. They give me something to concentrate on instead of my growing realization that this night with Trap will be my first with a total *man*.

I follow Trap's directions and use the soap. The shower's side jets have a lethal pressure. I lather and rinse my face, my arms, my belly.

"Wash your tits," Trap says, and I was foolish to think he wouldn't notice what I skipped.

"But the jet—" I start to say. If I finish the sentence, he'll ask me my color, and I already know I'll say green. So I soap my breasts, hoping Trap doesn't realize how small they are. The jet of water pounds my nipples exactly the way I feared it would, but the pain quickly ripens into something close to pleasure.

I wash my feet and my calves, knowing I'm ignoring Trap's demand to end with my toes. One glance confirms his tolerant smile; he understands exactly what I'm doing. My delay won't make a bit of difference in the long run.

I soap my shaved skin, nearly mesmerized by the new sensation. Before I can lose my nerve, I reach between my legs.

"Spread your lips," Trap says.

Obediently, I stretch my mouth into an O.

"Your pussy lips," he snaps. A wicked blush roasts my face, and for just a moment, I wonder if it's possible to faint from embarrassment.

To give myself time to recover, I roll the soap between my palms, slipping the bar over and over the mountains of suds. It squirts from my grasp, skating to the far corner of the shower. Instead of chasing after it, I ease my left hand between my legs. I use my index finger and my middle finger to part my folds. My right hand follows with the lather, slipping, sliding, smothering myself with foam.

"Rinse," Trap says, the word almost a groan.

I turn toward the jet that's targeted at my waist. I arch my back to frame the water's spray with my pelvis. Bracing myself for what I know I can't escape, I expose everything *down there* to the full force of the water.

Soap cascades down my thighs. My left hand plays the music it learned just a moment ago, my fingers angling, stretching. The jet pounds against me, pounds *into* me, a searing column of liquid heat.

My bottom grows tight. My hips push forward. My left hand splays wider, as if it's possible to bare more of me to the water. I realize my right hand is gripping my breast, cradling my aching nipple against my palm.

I want...

I need...

I'm so close...

I'm almost there...

And the jet of fire turns to a piercing spear of ice.

I yelp at the invasion, folding forward. My hands shoot out, blocking the freezing spray. My entire body trembles like I've just completed a marathon, and I barely find the coordination to turn toward the temperature controls.

Trap is there, his huge hand covering the lever. His message is clear: He's the person in control. He's the one who decides what I do and when and how I do it.

I start to shiver as he snaps, "Wash your asshole."

"Th— the water's too cold."

"Get the fucking soap."

The rainfall from above is freezing. The jet directed at my chest is a javelin. The one I rode below is a solid rod of ice.

My teeth start to chatter, but I cross the tile floor and retrieve the bar of soap. I roll it over my hands quickly. My fingers shake as I force myself back to the icy jets.

"P— please," I start to beg for an exception.

Trap's eyes are colder than the water. "Wash. Your. Asshole."

Humiliated, I spread my legs. I bend forward. I spread my cheeks with one hand and use the other to clean myself. My embarrassment is almost hot enough to counter the freezing water.

When the suds finally circle the drain, Trap turns off the spray on all three controls. I splutter and gasp, shuddering like a spent horse. Trap moves outside the tiled wall, only to return with a stack of terry towels. He hands me one and hangs the other two from hooks on the wall.

"Dry off," he says. "Then back to the bedroom. You're clean enough to fuck."

12

TRAP

I CIRCLE THE BED, TESTING THE LEATHER RESTRAINTS I'VE anchored at each corner. It never crossed my mind Ella would try to get off in there. She seems too...naive. Too pure. She doesn't have a clue how she looked in there.

The Beast cranks its vise around the base of my skull, but I argue I'm following the rules. Ella's clean now. She's safe.

The Beast says no. Ella took the reins. She managed her own pleasure. What will she do next? Touch me when I least expect it? I have to put her in her place. She has to know who's in control.

The Beast can gag on my ten-inch cock.

I talk a big game. But I know from past experience that the Beast can melt my rod with a single swipe of its slimy claws. It can kill a day-long hard-on with just one whisper about the worst memory in my life. It can lock me in a lightless room for days, weeks, months.

Fine. I'll do what I have to do. I'll show Ella who's boss.

She comes in from the bathroom, swaddled in a towel that covers her from chin to knees. She's done her best to dry her hair, tousling the ends till they curl above her tits. She looks vulnerable. Sweet.

I'm even gruffer than I need to be. "Drop the towel and get on the bed. On your back."

She climbs onto the mattress, giving me a clear view of her ass. My mouth fills with spit, and I barely resist the urge to bite her hard enough to mark.

Before I can imagine what the Beast would demand for that improvisation, Ella finds the middle of the bed. She's precise, like she calculated her spot with a tape measure. I've left her a pillow, a cradle so she can watch everything I do. I don't want her craning her neck.

She thinks she'll be safe there. She thinks she's out of harm's way. Her knees are pinned together like a Mother's Day corsage and her arms are two-by-fours nailed to her sides.

I stride to the headboard and snap my fingers. She jumps like I've fired a rifle. "Wrist," I order.

She closes her eyes, but she presents her hand. I close her into the cuff, tugging hard to make sure she can't free herself. The Beast demands its due because I touched another person, even a clean one, and I play a quick one-two-three-four-five on the headboard.

I walk around the bed and snap again. Good girl. Ella learns fast. I take the hand she offers and tighten the cuff, pulling a little harder than I have to. When I'm done, I trace my thumb across her palm, pressing just enough for her fingers to curl in. I'm making a promise. Or maybe I'm saying I'm sorry.

The Beast isn't impressed. It makes me answer twice, playing double penance above Ella's bird-like wrist.

At the foot of the bed, I snap for Ella's right foot, but her knees stay locked.

Impatient, I snap again.

Nothing.

"Ella," I warn, my voice liquid steel.

She whimpers a little, but she slides her heel across the bed. I'm vicious with the cuff, determined she'll never break free. The contact costs me another five notes, this time played against the footboard.

Ella's little rebellion is over by the time I reach her left foot. Her heel has already crossed the bed. She's waiting.

After she's secured, I run my index finger down her sole. Her foot twitches, and a shiver runs all the way up her leg. She smells clean, like rosemary and soap.

Of course, the Beast doesn't care. It makes me pay for the contact, three times for good measure.

Ella's pussy is bare to the world, flawless orchid folds beneath her swollen clit. Her breath catches, and my attention is dragged from the paradise between her legs to her face. The flush of the shower has faded from her cheeks. Tiny folds crease her forehead.

"Color?" I ask, almost choking on the fear that I've already pushed her too far, too fast.

She swallows hard and I think she'll tap out. But then she whispers, "Green."

My good girl. My good, brave girl.

My cock surges, heavy as an anvil.

The Beast mutters in my ear, insisting Ella can't be trusted. If I had any other woman in my bed, I'd circle around to the nightstand now and take out a pair of gloves—black silk to keep me clean. Safe. I'd climb onto the bed. I'd kneel between my clean girl's legs and use my covered hand to…

The Beast says fuck that. I have to make sure Ella knows who's in charge.

My cock thinks the Beast is on to something. Usually, it has to wait its turn. Ladies first, after all. But tonight, it's heavy as a log, my heart buried somewhere deep inside, pounding a drum-beat that shakes my balls.

I tear off my shirt. I rip the belt from my jeans. I shove my boxers to the floor and free my eager dick. The Beast crows its approval.

Scrambling onto the bed, I ignore Ella's gasp of surprise. I spit into my right hand and close it around my eager cock. My left hand clutches my balls, squeezing hard enough to make even the Beast happy.

I stroke myself from root to tip, my fingers tight. My breath comes in short, sharp huffs like I've just come off a six-minute mile.

Ella pulls away, stretching toward the far side of the bed, but I did my job well. There's no way she's escaping. I want to tell her this is the only way I can keep her safe, the only way I can appease the Beast, but it will take too long to say the words, and she might never believe me anyway.

Another stroke, a vicious tug, hating myself, healing myself. One more, and my balls seize up, high and tight and hard as baseballs. I bellow as I pull again, a wordless shout of rage and glory.

I come.

Spunk arcs from my cock to Ella's belly. She freezes at the first hot splash, and then I paint her, thick shiny cords lashing her soft, clean flesh.

She's mine. She's helpless. I'm the one in absolute control.

I work my cock until I'm pumped dry, until I shiver, until I'm ashamed. I crash forward on hands and knees, my head hovering over Ella's belly. The bleachy smell of cum drowns out my sweet girl's rosemary and soap.

The Beast is cackling like a hyena. I brace myself to ask Ella her color, to find out if this is the end of our night together.

But when I find her eyes, they're gleaming. Her frown has somehow transformed into a brilliant, close-lipped smile. She looks like someone has told her a secret. Like she just learned the punchline to an ancient, dirty joke.

"Green," she says, before I can ask. "Oh my God, green."

13

ALIX

~

I SHOULD BE DISGUSTED. I ENTERED TRAP'S BEDROOM THE cleanest I've ever been in my life. Now, I'm a filthy mess, a woman's who's been used like a lifeless sponge.

And I'm happier than I've ever been in bed with a man.

I made him that excited. *I* pushed him beyond his control.

I don't think he even realized the things he was saying, the words he chanted as he hulked over me. Eff me. Eff himself. Eff the effing eff in his brain.

But that moment when he actually reached his climax? He was free. He was broken and open and almost blindingly pure.

I can smell his semen on my skin. It's like sunshine and fresh-cut grass and it makes the creature *down there* more than a little crazy.

As soon as I give him my color, he climbs off the bed. He yanks open his nightstand drawer and pulls out a pair of gloves. They're black fabric, the sort of thing a serial killer would wear.

But Trap's not a killer. Trap's a man wrestling with some

horrific trauma. I want to tell him not to use the gloves, to try touching me without them, but I'm not his therapist. I'm not so naive that I think pleasuring himself over my body will cure his compulsive state forever.

He mounts the bed again, climbing over my leg so that he's kneeling in the triangle between my thighs. He rests his weight on his forearms, bringing his face so close I think he's going to kiss me.

I squirm, desperate to cover myself with my hands. Jason said I was smelly *down there*. I can't imagine why Trap would possibly want to stare at me. But this is one of the things he told me about in the kitchen. I don't understand why he wants to do this, but I'm ready.

He taps me, and my body tries to jump three feet into the air, stopped only by the bonds on my wrists and ankles.

I guess I wasn't really ready.

"What—" I start to say, but he's doing it again, tapping the most private part of me.

He sets a rhythm, steady and fast. He flutters his fingers, one to the next to the next, like his compulsion ritual but faster. Then he settles into a steady, insistent drumbeat—*tap, tap, tap.*

"Oh my God," I say without thinking. "That feels amazing."

"Good, Ella. Talk to me. Tell me what you like."

I don't have words for that. But he shifts back to triplets, and my ankles strain against their bonds. I want to close my knees because the things he's doing are too intense. I want to keep my knees open forever.

I have to move. I can't move. He tied me to the bed, and I let him do it without a word of protest.

I'm bad. Dirty. I should tell him to stop. I should tell him we're done.

He drops a finger, or maybe it's his thumb, on the sensitive ridge of flesh between my front and back. The weight is amazing. It stretches me *down there*. It makes every touch at the front echo through my body, every tap of his finger.

The hungry animal inside me insists I arch my hips. I know that puts my private parts closer to his face, which he must find disgusting, but I can't stop myself.

"Please," I beg, tears leaking from my eyes.

"More," I plead.

"Faster. Faster. Faster."

My toes point. My calves stretch. My thighs petrify into stone.

This is better than the water jet in the shower. This is better than anything I ever did with Jason. This is better than any dream I've ever had of helping myself, of freeing myself, of unlocking the door to pleasure.

I'm close, so close. My head thrashes. My fingers curl into fists, fighting to break free from the headboard.

Trap delivers a single, devastating tap.

The creature inside me pulls into a tiny, fur-wrapped ball.

Another tap.

The creature whines.

One more tap.

The creature explodes, gasping and flailing, firing every neuron in my brain at the chaotic speed of light. I'm clutching, I'm gasping, I'm screaming an endless, everlasting *YES!*

I ride the waves back to my body, back to the bed. Trap hasn't stopped. His fingers still work their impossible magic, softer and gentler, tapping flesh too sensitive to tolerate his attention.

No. Not too sensitive.

Just sensitive enough.

My body pulls together, tighter, tighter, tighter, and this time when I explode, I fall through an endless pile of cotton clouds.

After a century, sensation rushes back to my ankles and my wrists. I can feel a thousand tiny abrasions where I struggled against my bonds. My right calf twitches, threatening to seize up in a painful cramp, but I flex my foot and it subsides.

Once I asked Leo was meth was like. He thought a long

time, and then he said, "Like sex with a person who knows what you need before you even think to ask for it."

I pretended like I knew what he was talking about.

Now, I finally do. And maybe for the first time in my life, I understand why my brother is an addict.

"Oh my God," I say, and my voice sounds very far away. "That was amazing." I force myself to open my eyes. "*You're* amazing," I say to Trap.

He's sitting back on his heels, eyeing me with a smug grin. "Welcome back," he says.

"I never…" I struggle to sit up. Somehow I'm still bound to the bed. It seems like the restraints should have incinerated when my mind left my body.

"Okay," I say, and my voice is a little steadier. "I need to clean up. I'm a mess."

"You're perfect," he says, and he runs his gloved fingers down the inside of my thigh. I can feel the streak of wetness he leaves behind, *my* wetness, and I consider dying of embarrassment.

"Come on," I say. "Let me go."

"No." His voice is steady. Absolute. He's back in full command. "Not yet. We're only starting to play."

14

TRAP

SHE HAS HER SAFEWORD IF SHE REALLY WANTS ME TO FREE HER.

The sight of her pussy quivering in aftershock makes my cock twitch. I catch the moment she realizes I'm staring at her snatch. There's the blush I've come to expect, the hot wash of color over her cheeks.

I've never heard a woman scream the way she did when she came. She said she wasn't a virgin, and I took her at her word. But I'll bet the entire freeport that was the first time she ever had an orgasm.

It won't be the last.

I climb off the bed and make my way to the bathroom. Behind me, I hear her little mew of disbelief, and I smile. The towel I want is hanging beside the sink, but I take my time slipping it from the bar.

"Trap?" she calls. And then, with a little more urgency, "Trap!"

I run water in the sink, soaking half the hand towel. I use

my left hand, letting my silk glove flood with water. I keep my right hand free. I don't want to wash away the scent of Ella's pussy.

She's panting as I come back to the bedroom, yanking at the bonds that hold her wrists. "Hush," I say, the terrycloth hot and heavy in my hand.

She's a good girl. She falls silent the second I climb onto the bed.

A drop of warm water falls from the towel to her belly, rolling into the sweet divot of her navel. I want to trace its path with my tongue, but the Beast would throw a fit.

Instead, I wash my Ella clean.

Some of my come has dried, flaking like pearly glitter. The thicker ropes, though, are still liquid—heavy and sticky. I clean her belly first, using broad swipes of the towel. The terry and my gloves keep the Beast at bay.

The towel is warm, but Ella's clean belly cools quickly. I measure the temperature by the peaks of her nips—two bullets rising out of soft brown targets.

I wash her small tits, bunching the towel so I can make quick, short strikes. She moans at the attention, arching her back like she's offering me a feast, but I know I can't indulge. Her head falls back on the pillow and her knees twitch, trying to draw together.

Pinching her left nipple between folds of cloth, I tighten my fingers to scrub away the last of my come, twisting hard to do the job right. She gasps, and her eyes fly open.

"Yellow!" she barks.

I pull back immediately, dropping my towel-covered hand to the thousand-count sheet. My good, good girl, keeping herself safe.

Some twisted part of me, something deep inside my lizard brain, is grateful she used the safeword. If she said *yellow* now then I can have faith she'll say *red* when she needs to. I can push her. I can trust her. The Beast won't win tonight.

"I'm sorry," she says. "I shouldn't have—"

"Stop." I cut her off. "You did exactly the right thing."

"It was just so intense. My erogenous zones have never been so sensitive."

She sounds like she's reporting symptoms to a doctor. From the blush on her cheeks, she feels about as sexy as a hospital patient, too.

I want to scrub the formal words from her mind. I want to tear her down to single syllables—tits and nips, clit and cunt, cock and balls and hard, hot, fuck.

"I'm sorry," she says again, and a desperate panic rattles beneath her words. She doesn't want to leave my bed. She's not ready to be done.

"No apologies," I say. "Breathe."

She takes in a short, sharp gasp.

"No," I say. "Relax. *Breathe.*" I take my own deep breath, showing her how it's done. My cock thinks I'm calling a meeting; I'm hard again, and I can't imagine how much I'd ache if I hadn't shot my load before I started playing with fire.

"That's right," I say, as she imitates me. "You're fine. You're safe. Keep that up. I'll be right back."

I take the towel back to the bathroom and collect another one from the rack. Soft terry. Warm water. I know exactly how to finish the job now.

"There you go," I say, returning to find her exhaling on a four count. "I'm almost done here. I promise this won't hurt."

I wash her right tit like I'm polishing an opal—soft, soft, feather-soft swipes. Her nip gets just as dark as the one I pinched, just as hard, but I treat it like a treasure. Just a touch on the side... A brush across the top... A soft, sweet stroke all around.

Her breath catches and, out of the corners of my eyes, I see her hands curl into fists. She's so responsive, so tightly strung...

If I were a normal man, I'd take that nip in my mouth. I'd roll it with my tongue. I'd suck on it hard, then soft, letting her moans tell me just how much she can take. I'd get her so turned on she'd *beg* to feel my teeth. I'd wedge my knee in the hot, wet V between her legs, give her something to ride while I pinched the left side, bit the right side, taking away the burn with my hot, wet tongue. I'd stretch her. Pull her. Back away and laugh as she begged and then I'd flick her with my fingers, again, again, again until she opened beneath me, folded around me, coming hot and hard and heavy, screaming my name.

Fuck.

I'm not normal; the Beast sees to that. But I'm hard as a diamond, my cock aching with every pulse of my heart.

Ella's clean now.

Safe.

And with my soft touch and her sensitive *erogenous zones*, she's ready for anything I need.

It's time now—even the Beast agrees.

I take the towel back to the bathroom and slap it down beside the sink. My hard-on is in charge now, making it difficult to think. It pulls me back to the bed.

I intend to go straight to my dresser, to the bottom drawer with its collection tools, but I make the mistake of looking at the wall of windows. The sun has set. It's dark outside. I can't make out a hint of the patio, the lawn, the distant line of trees.

All I can see is Ella. My Ella. Spread-eagled and waiting. Her legs must be getting tired now. Her arms must be starting to ache. She's raising her head from her pillow, and she's watching me, waiting for me, trusting me.

The windows blur her beauty. They turn her skin to gold. They darken the shadow of her pussy so I can't make out the dark pink home it's time to claim as mine.

The Beast growls, making sure I haven't forgotten its rules.

I tear my gaze away from the windows and yank open the dresser drawer. My right glove is slick with Ella, the left with the water I used to bathe her. It's almost time to take them off. Almost time to be free.

I stare at all the tools the Beast has taught me to use.

"What are you doing?" Ella calls from the bed.

She's a good girl. She deserves to know. I lift the box out of the drawer and carry it over to the bed.

My cock is as hot as a fireplace poker and every bit as hard. It twitches when I take out the string of foil packets that will keep it safe.

I show Ella the rubbers, and her face floods with relief. I can read her so easily now, pick up on all of her emotions. I know the way her mind works. Any man who thinks of protection at a time like this is a man who can be trusted.

The box has tools for other times, other uses. I take out the gag, the one I told her I'd use, when we talked down in the kitchen. The silicone ball floats in its leather harness, looking big enough to choke her. I've changed my mind. She's already said *yellow* once, and I need her mouth free to say it again.

Setting aside the gag, I show her the dildo. Its ridged rubber is half again as large as my own huge cock, traced with massive veins designed to push against her clit. Ella's eyes grow wide, and she shrinks away. I could teach her. I could coach her. I could get her to take the whole damn thing, but that won't give me the release I need tonight.

I put the dildo back and take out the vibrator. It doesn't try to look real; it's got a bulb no woman could manage and a panel with three speeds, along with a snaking electric cord so it never gets tired. Ella looks interested, and for a heartbeat I consider giving her what she wants, but my cock jerks hard, and the vibrator goes back in the drawer too.

My fingers close around the tool I need. I'm not sure Ella will recognize it. I don't want to scare her. I hope it won't hurt her. Because this is what the Beast commands.

The black rubber looks evil. The ridges look hard. It looks longer and thicker and far more brutal than any body can take. The flared base is as wide as my palm, a mercy, another way of keeping her safe, but Ella might not understand.

I take out the lube first. She needs to know I'll help.

I didn't think my cock could get harder, but it's had enough with my delays. Steeling myself with a steady breath, I meet Ella's trusting gaze.

And I show her the butt plug she needs to take before she's clean enough, safe enough that the Beast will let me fuck her sweet little cunt.

15

ALIX

∼

"No."

The word is out of my mouth before I can stop it. It's like my body is completely separated from the brain that came up with the whole "we're saying *yes* to everything tonight" idea. My arms try to contract, to cross over my chest, even though I can't move an inch. My hips rotate in as my knees fight to touch. Every cell in my body rejects that rubber monster instinctively.

Trap flips open the cap on the tube he showed me. It's lubricant, and he squirts a generous dollop on top of that black nightmare. I shake my head more vehemently. There's no way that thing can fit inside my vagina.

I find my words. "You didn't tell me about this downstairs."

He didn't. He told me I'd have to wash. He said he'd tie me to the bed. He said I'd orgasm—*come*, he said—when he touched me. But he didn't say he'd impale me with that terrifying black thing.

"You're right," he says. "I should have. But I didn't want to scare you. You can take this. I'd never ask you to do something you aren't capable of doing. You already know I'll slow down when you need me to."

I shake my head again. "No."

But I don't say *yellow*.

And I don't say *red*.

I want him to know I'm scared. I want him to know I've never had anything close to that size inside me. I want him to set it aside, to say it's a joke, to say he really means to use his own impressive thing, that's the way we'll make love.

But he's told me the rules. I know the way to make him stop, and it's not by saying *no*. *No* doesn't count. In this room, *no* is the same as *yes*.

"Please," I say. "Don't put that thing inside me."

I mean the words. I don't want it anywhere near me. But I realize this is part of what *he* needs—me pleading with him. He needs me to pretend I want him to stop.

I pull on my bonds, acting like I want to get away from him. His thing leaps like I've touched it. He's excited by my pretended fear.

And so am I.

I know I can stop him any time; he proved that when he hurt my breast. So I can afford to play this game now. "Please," I beg. "It's too much."

That's true. And there are more true things I can say. "I've never done this before. I don't know what sort of woman you usually bring here, but I don't do this kind of thing."

The words tumble out, faster and faster. I breathe harder, like I'm terrified.

I'm ashamed to admit it, but this game is…fun. There's power in saying the words, in playing the role. Now I understand why my safeword isn't *no*, why we aren't using *stop*. When I'm certain I'm safe, certain I'm in control, it's exciting to pretend he's forcing me.

"You can't," I say, purposely breaking my voice, like I'm sobbing. "Please. Let me go. I promise I won't tell anyone."

Trap is kneeling between my legs. His thing is engorged. He's more excited than I've seen him tonight, and that makes me excited too. He puts a hand under my thigh, spreading me even wider than the cuffs around my ankles. He slides his fingers up, spreading them, supporting me, supporting my bottom until I'm arched as far off the bed as I can possibly be.

"Don't make me do this," I plead. "I'll do anything else. Anything you ask. Just not this. Please, please, please…"

He shoves the black rubber against my anus.

I yelp.

The sound pops out of me, like I'm a dog or maybe a seal. I thrash in my bonds, really fighting, really trying to get away.

My *bottom*? He thinks he can put that thing inside my *butt*?

He must be surprised by my fighting because he swears, combinations of words I've never heard before. He's calling me a beast, which doesn't make sense. An effing, GD beast.

His swearing doesn't make sense. His gloved grip on my thigh doesn't make sense. His thinking he can fit that monster rubber *thing* in my butt doesn't make sense.

Yellow. The word's right there. I can say it.

But I don't want to.

He gave me my first orgasm ever. He made my body do things it's never done for anyone else.

I owe him.

And I want to make him happy.

And if he thinks I can take that thing, then he must be right.

I make a conscious effort to stop pulling away. I try to relax my legs. I do my best to ease the trembling that's taken over my arms.

"Good girl," he says.

I've never wanted to be anyone's *girl*. I'm a woman. A grown, thinking, perfectly competent woman.

But when Trap says *girl*, I know exactly what he means. He's taking care of me. He's protecting me. He's helping me be the best person I can be.

He brings the rubber back to my bottom. Every muscle from my belly to my knees squeezes tight in rebellion. I can't help it. It's like my body knows what he's asking his wrong. Is impossible.

"Relax," he says, pressing steadily.

"If you think this is easy, then *you* try it!" I'm as surprised as he is when I snap. Our little game is over.

He chuckles and pushes harder.

It hurts.

Without my giving my body permission, it tries to squirm away. I can only move a few inches in any direction. My arms are really shaking now, like I've been out in a snowstorm for hours. My hips flex left, then right, desperate to escape his grasp.

"Just…stay…still!"

He's more determined than ever and fire sears inside me and I know how much this much means to him and my body can't stretch anymore and there must be a reason he's doing this and I'm splitting in two and he's hollering again and I'm tearing apart and he calls me a beast and this will never end and it hurts, it hurts, it hurts…

"Red!" I shout, knowing that if he doesn't stop, I'll die.

16

TRAP

SHE SCREAMS OUT *RED*, AND EVERYTHING FREEZES.

I'm a monster. I'm broken. I'm twisted and sick. A normal man would be grateful for everything she's already given. He'd wrap his cock and plow her cunt and shoot his wad, grateful for the chance to have a woman like Ella in his bed in the first place.

The Beast says I can't do that.

The Beast says Ella has to be clean.

The Beast says Ella has to take the plug.

Red.

I need to plug her ass.

Red.

I need to prove that I'm the one in control, I'm the one who makes the rules, I'm the one who decides who can and cannot fuck.

Red.

I need to scrub the Beast out of my life, I need to strangle it, shred it, kill it fucking forever.

Red.

Kill the Beast. Kill the Beast. Kill the Beast.

Red.

17

ALIX

FOR A MOMENT, TRAP KEEPS PUSHING, AND THE SWORD CUTTING me in two keeps burning. My throat is torn from screaming *red*. My nose is running. My eyes stream.

Through my tears, I can see Trap's face. His mouth twists around horrible words. His eyes are on fire, a rim of flame around pupils so wide I wonder if he's drugged.

He kneels there, magically turned to stone. His hands don't move. His arms don't move. He's balanced on the edge of a ravine so deep I can't imagine the floor.

And then, with a bellow like an elephant dying in a pit, he pulls that thing out of me and throws it across the room.

Gasping for breath, he fumbles at the bonds around my left ankle. His fingers slip, and he tries again; he squares his shoulders and makes one more try.

My left leg is free. My right. He scrambles to the top of the bed and releases my right wrist. Hurries around to free my left.

It hurts to bring my arms to my sides; they burn like they'll never move that way again. I want to be brave; I want to be good, but a sob rips out of my throat.

Trap is back; I didn't even realize he'd left the room. He's holding a glass of water in one hand, and there's a sky-colored blanket draped over the opposite arm. I really must be out of it, because I didn't even see when he pulled on a pair of boxers. He's taken off his gloves, too.

He puts the water on his nightstand and climbs onto the bed with the blanket. I try to move, intending to give him room, but every muscle in my body protests. I settle for curling into a ball.

He whispers something, nonsense sounds, the type of things a jockey mutters to a frightened horse. He unfolds the blanket and covers me, which is when I realize I'm shivering hard, my teeth clattering together like a bad Halloween toy.

"You're safe," he says, tucking the blanket in closer. "You're fine." He repeats the words, over and over, like a child's spell against monsters in the dark.

"I— I'm c—cold," I say, or try to shape the words with my clumsy lips.

He scoots up to the headboard, retrieving the pillow that was under my head and stashing it behind his back. He leans toward me, and I'm not sure if he lifts me, or if I crawl toward him, but suddenly I'm cradled against his body.

My spine curls against his belly, only the blanket between us. I sit in the V of his bowed legs, my knees tucked almost beneath my chin. His arms fold around me and my head nestles in the hollow between his chin and his shoulder. He squeezes me tight, supporting me with his arms and legs. The blanket feels like a cloud between us.

"You're fine," he whispers. "You're safe. My good, good girl."

When I finally stop shivering, he leans away and I manage to whimper a protest. But he's only reaching toward the nightstand. He brings me the glass of water, tilting it gently so I can take one swallow, two, and then he lets me drain the whole thing with greedy little grasps.

He leans away again, and this time I believe he'll be back. He fumbles for something beneath the lamp, and he comes back with a golden packet the length of his thumb. Reaching around me, keeping me close, he fiddles with it until he's released a tantalizing dark-brown square, which he promptly breaks in two.

He places one of the pieces between my lips, centering it on my fledgling tongue, and the taste of chocolate shoots to the base of my brain. It's creamy and dark, with notes of coffee and smoke and just a hint of the berries he fed me a lifetime ago.

When it's melted, he feeds me the rest of the square, and another whole piece after that. I feel each individual molecule of the chocolate hit my bloodstream. My brain comes online, module by module. Fingers. Toes. Arms. Legs. Motions. Memories. Words.

"What was it?" I finally ask. "What *happened* to make you need that?"

He stiffens beneath me. He already answered my question, at least in part—back at Debasement a lifetime ago, when I was trying to decide if it was safe to get in his car. He was hurt as a child. I understand that. But I have to know more—what kind of hurt. What made him be this way. When he stays silent, I ask, "Why are you *so* afraid to touch?"

I think he'll pretend not to hear me. Pretend not to understand. Maybe he'll distract me with another piece of chocolate or a second glass of water.

But he shakes his head, a single terse twitch. "Not touch," he says after a long pause. "I'm not afraid to touch. I'm afraid of germs."

Mysophobia, my brain immediately supplies. I can picture the page in my freshman year *Abnormal Psychology* textbook—the cycle of compensating behaviors that get worse and worse when the root cause is left untreated.

"Germs," I say, so he knows I'm listening. I hope he knows I care. I don't want to push him, but he said the word out loud and from the weary disgust in his voice, he's been holding it in for a very long time.

He says, "I told you I touched something when I was a kid."

He hesitates for long enough that I think he's changed his mind. Afraid of shutting him down completely, I wait. And wait. And wait.

"I was twelve," he finally says. "My parents got divorced the year before. I did screwy things after they split. I'd sort my base-ball cards for hours, like if I got them in the perfect order, Mom and Dad would get back together. I had a ritual for eating, all the red things first, then green, white, brown. I had a plan for bedtime—take a shower for exactly five minutes, read exactly five pages of a book, turn my pillow over exactly five times."

"You were trying to control your environment."

"My mother would have agreed with you. Dad called me a faggot and told me to get my shit together."

"That wasn't fair!"

"Dad wasn't real big on fair."

He falls silent again, and I wonder what memories he's working through. I hate the fact that he suffered as a child. I want to find his father and tell him off.

Trap goes on, like I've actually figured out something useful to say. "Dad had a major business opportunity come up, in DRC, Congo, and he decided to take me with him. I didn't know it at the time, but he broke his custody arrangement with Mom. On the plane, he said he was going to toughen me up. Make me a man."

"You must have been terrified!"

"He was my father." Trap's voice is bitter, like he needs to spit. "He had to know what was best."

Another pause, this one the longest yet. Even through the blanket, I can feel the tension in Trap's body. His chest is as tight as the corners on a hospital bed. His fingers clench and release like he's scrubbing filthy laundry in a stream.

He's said all he can. He can't push himself more. So *I* do the pushing. I ask, "What happened?"

He sighs, and I never knew human lungs could hold so much air. "Dad had a couple of business partners—two guys from South Africa who scared the shit out of me. All the white men were armed—rifles to cover the workers, with handguns just in case. People—children—hauled tons of earth out of holes fifty feet deep, day after day after day…"

"What were they doing?"

"Mining diamonds."

Diamonds. Like Diamond Freeport.

"How long were you there?"

"Less than a year." He seems grateful for the easy answer. But then he says, "The mine was shut down. Quarantined. There was an Ebola breakout, and ninety-seven workers died."

"Oh my God!"

"My father decided it was time to bug out. But first he stole from his partners—a ten-pound bag of the finest diamonds the mine produced."

"Ten pounds—" I start to say. Not much. Not worth haunting Trap for decades.

"Cut and polished, worth about a hundred mill."

I'm too shocked to respond.

But he's rolling now. "One hundred million dollars. In a kid's backpack. *My* backpack."

"The partners caught you with the diamonds?"

He shakes his head. "My father hid me where he knew they'd never look."

I wait. He seems to think I already know the answer.

When I can't come up with anything, he blows a short breath through stiff lips. "He put me in the morgue."

"Oh, Trap!"

"He put me in the aluminum hut where they stored the

bodies. He left me with my backpack, five gallons of water, and a stack of army surplus field rations."

"But *Ebola*. How did you survive? Isn't it one of the most contagious viruses in the world?"

"Only if you touch a corpse. It isn't transmitted by air."

"You poor…" I'm too horrified to finish. I start to imagine the heat, the stench, the *terror*… I try to stop before I'm overwhelmed.

"He taped out a square on the floor. He told me not to move outside it, no matter what happened. He said if I did, I'd die bleeding from every hole in my body. He told me to wait for him, and he'd be back when the coast was clear."

"And did he? Come back?"

Trap shakes his head. "Ten days later, the spacemen came."

"Spacemen?"

"Relief workers, in hazmat suits."

"What happened to your father?"

I feel him shrug, the same one-shoulder twitch I thought was casual in Debasement. "He was in the field hospital when the relief workers found me, already in a coma. He died the next day."

"What happened to *you*?"

"They kept me in quarantine for a month. Then they passed me from government agent to government agent. I didn't have a passport or visa. Dad had greased palms every step of the way to get us in country. I think they finally sent me home because I was too fucking weird to keep around."

I'm offended for the lost and frightened child he'd been. "How were you weird?"

"I already had a bunch of bad habits before I left—the baseball cards, the eating, the bedtime crap. While I was in the morgue, I came up with more. If I tapped my canteen five times, the water would be safe. If I stirred the MRE five times, the food couldn't hurt me. It was stupid. But I thought it saved my life."

"Compulsions aren't stupid."

His lips quirk in a bitter smile. "Seventeen years later, those same *compulsions* rule my life. The Beast. That's what I call them, in my mind. The goddamn animal that keeps me alive. That keeps me crazy."

Beast. He hadn't been calling *me* a beast. He'd been wrestling with the tics that keep him sane.

I make my voice as gentle as I can. "So, what happened tonight?"

"Tonight? Tonight, I tried to celebrate the biggest business milestone of my life with a beautiful, willing partner."

My cheeks heat, and I'm glad I don't have to meet his gaze. I don't think we could have had a word of this conversation actually facing each other. "Until I freaked out," I say.

"This was some pretty messed-up shit," he says.

"But you told me the rules downstairs. None of it came as a surprise."

He huffs a short laugh. "None of it?"

"Okay," I amend. "Some of it." I let my admission sit between us for a minute. But then I ask, "What happened, though? What changed?" I start to sit up, to pull away from his broad chest. "How can you stand to sit here with my head on your shoulder?"

He reaches across with one hand and presses me back to my place. His palm is gentle on my head. His fingers tangle in my hair. "The Beast doesn't seem important anymore. Not when it threatened someone more scared than I was. Seventeen years was long enough. I don't need it anymore."

I love the warmth of his hand and the firmness of his chest. But I have to dispute his words. "Phobias don't work that way. People don't just snap their fingers and say, 'I'm done.'"

"Who the fuck knows?" he says. "Maybe when I wake up tomorrow, I'll be back to square one. But I pushed you too far, and the Beast couldn't care less. *You* trusted me. *You* needed me. So, screw the Beast. I'm done."

I want it to be that simple. I want him to feel as safe as he's making me feel.

I suspect it's going to take more than a single conversation for him to process everything he's feeling. But it seems cruel to make him say more tonight.

I don't want to leave here. I don't want to give up this circle of comfort. I have to keep him talking about *something*, so I reach back to the heart of the story he's just told me. "What happened to the diamonds?" I ask. "The ones your father gave you?"

18

TRAP

I WAVE MY HAND, DOING MY BEST TO TAKE IN THE ROOM, THE house, the entire goddamn freeport. "You're looking at 'em."

"What?" She sounds confused.

"No one takes away a kid's backpack when it's the only thing he owns. And there's no security to speak of, on a military flight out of Congo. Mom never asked what I brought home, and I was smart enough to keep my mouth shut till I was old enough to use them. My father's diamonds, a hundred mill... They're Diamond Freeport now."

The admission feels good. Right. No one else knows how I started this business. I'm glad Ella knows the truth.

Which makes me realize how much I want to make things right with her. How much I want to give her what *she* wants. What she needs, now that the Beast is dead and gone.

I work my fingers through her hair, making my way to the nape of her neck. When I knead the tiny muscles there, she purrs like a kitten. I lower my head to whisper by her ear, "What would make you feel good?"

She stiffens, for just a moment. I wouldn't have felt it if her entire body hadn't been curled against mine. Before I can react, though, she says, "What you're doing right now is pretty amazing."

It's a coy voice, and I should probably drop my question, but I really feel I owe her. She spent the past four hours with the biggest asshole in the known universe. I want to prove to her—and maybe to myself too—that I actually know how to make a woman happy.

"Don't tell me you're getting shy now," I tease. My fingertips skate past her tits and down her belly, pausing over the mound she shaved for me. I brush against that soft smooth skin, and she shudders.

She whispers, so quiet I can barely hear, "I like it when you touch me down there."

"Down there?" I say, starting to laugh until I realize she's serious.

Indignantly, she says, "I don't have as much experience as you do."

I keep my voice light. "Then tell me what you like."

She shakes her head.

"Then tell me something that worked tonight. Something we did before…" *Before I tried to ream your ass with a horse-size butt plug.* I don't say that last part out loud, of course.

She covers her face with both hands. I feel her rocking, just a little, shifting back and forth like she needs to run away.

"Ella?" I ask, closing gentle fingers around her wrist.

"I'm not—" she starts to say, but she stops herself. It seems forever before she finally comes up with, "I'm not good at this. I don't know what to say."

"Bullshit."

"I'm scared!"

"Of what? You were brave enough to get in my car. You

were horny enough to get in my bed. Why is it so terrifying to tell me what you want?"

"I don't know the words!"

She shouts, and I'm stunned.

"I don't know what to say!" she gasps. "You'll think I'm desperate. Or stupid. I don't want to sound disgusting or crude."

My sweet, good girl… "There's nothing you can say that will make me think less of you," I assure her.

She moans, still hiding behind the screen of her hands.

"Ella…" I cajole, but that only makes it worse. She's pulling inside herself, shrinking away. Her pulse pounds beneath my fingertips like she's a jackrabbit fighting a snare.

I'm losing her. I have to say something. Do something. So I try the only thing I can think of before she falls apart completely.

Gently, determined not to hurt her, I pull her palm from her face. I shift my grip on her wrist, moving my fingers to weave between hers. I guide our hands down her body, ignoring the sudden intake of her breath. Squeezing her fingers beneath mine, I say, "This is your *tit*."

I push the word as I say it, purposely making it short. Sharp. I squeeze again, like that will help her remember.

Moving my fingers with hers, I pinch them together, tweaking her hard enough to get her attention. "This is your nip."

When I pull our hands south, she resists just a little. She knows where we're going, and she has to be afraid. But I cup her firmly, and she has no choice but to do the same. "This is your mound."

We move lower. "Your clit," I say, and she gasps when we slide our knuckles over the firm little knob.

We part her lips. She's wet there, soaking, and I almost breathe a prayer of thanks, because if she hated me for touching her, I don't know what I'd do. "Your pussy," I say, circling our fingers around her opening.

She whines a little, a sweet needy whimper, and I slip one of her fingers inside. "Your slit." I add mine next to hers, both of us dipping together. "Your snatch." Again, as her spine melts against me and she offers up a perfect little moan. "Your cunt."

I move our soaked fingers lower, following the slick path she's already made for herself. "Your taint," I say, gliding front to back, once, twice, a third time.

Her thighs grow tight above our still-joined hands. I want to give her what she's asking for. But more than that, I want to set her free. So I take our sticky fingers and brush them over the tight rosebud I savaged earlier tonight. "Your ass," I whisper.

Before she can think about it, I lean to my left, shifting her weight to my thigh. I guide our hands inside the fly of my boxers. Cupping her hand in mine, I press against the cotton, stretching to reach low. "My balls," I say, showing her how to squeeze them. "My nuts."

I'm hard now, long and heavy. Hands together, I guide her in stroking me from root to tip. "My cock," I say. And just in case she missed the point, we tug it again. "My dick."

I squeeze her fingers in mine, feeling every knuckle around my cock. "We fuck," I say. "I go down on you. I eat you out. You give me a blowjob. A handjob."

You take it up the ass. I don't say that. Not tonight.

Instead, I say, "We come."

She needed to hear the words. But I needed to feel them— every single one. I needed to touch her, every inch, to confirm the Beast is nowhere in sight.

Not once did I flinch. Not once did I feel the urge to count, to tap, to play.

Whatever Ella says about phobias and therapy and the impossibility of instant cures, I'm free.

I pull her back to rest against my chest. I raise her hand to my lips. It's still sticky, her juices caught in the web between her fingers. I suck them clean one by one, tracing them with my tongue.

When I'm done, I place my still-damp thumb against the soft O of her mouth. She opens for me with a greedy little gasp. I fuck her lips with my thumb as she sucks me clean and only after she swallows do I bend down to her ear.

I exhale softly and wait for her to shudder. Then I whisper, "Tell me how to fuck you. Tell me what you want."

19

ALIX

"I WANT..."

The two words hang there.

I want to say more. I want to use the words Trap gave me.

But I've been silent for so many years.

Jason and I had sex every Saturday night, because we weren't too tired from the workweek, and we didn't have class the next day. He thanked me like a gentleman, and he wiped me dry with Kleenex, every single time.

"Ella..." Trap says.

I should tell him the truth. I should tell him my name is Alix.

But Ella's the woman who went to Debasement. Ella's the one who dared to visit this castle in the woods. Ella let a stranger do incredible things to her, with her.

Ella's the one who came.

I swallow hard, and then I decide Ella can do this too. Ella can trust. Ella can say, *does* say, "I want you to go down on me." I don't fly apart in a million pieces from embarrassment. So I go on. "I want you to eat me out. And then I want you to f— fuck me with your cock. Hard. I want you to squeeze my tits and suck my nips and fuck me till I come."

The room is silent, except for the pounding of my heart. I stare at my twisted fingers—the fingers that found my pussy, the ones that have been in Trap's mouth. But I can't sit like a statue forever.

I twist around until I'm facing him. I force myself to raise my head, to find his eyes. I see the wild jungle there, hot and dark and full of life.

He reaches out one of his giant hands. He doesn't hesitate. Doesn't flinch. He cups my face, his touch impossibly gentle. "Good girl," he says.

And then he rises on all fours. He closes his hands around my ankles and tugs me toward the foot of the bed, sending the cloud-soft blanket over the edge of the bed.

He growls like a wild animal, and my pussy squeezes hard with desire. He runs his hands up my thighs, and I know I'm supposed to open to him.

I want to. I trust him. But I can't help myself. As my knees fall to either side, I cover myself with my hands.

He traces my legs like I've given him a present. His thumbs find the exhausted hollows behind my knees. He follows the lines of long muscle, stroking my thighs until I start to melt.

"Please," he says, settling his fingertips in the creases at the tops of my legs. "Let me look at you, Ella."

A sound comes out of me, part exasperation, part laugh. He could force me to move my hands. He could make me do anything he wants.

But this isn't about what Trap wants. This is about what I need.

I shift my hands to the bed, clutching the sheet on either side of my hips. It takes all of my willpower to keep from slamming my knees together.

"Such a sweet pussy," Trap says, staring at me like I'm something beautiful. "Such a brave girl."

I'm proud when he says it. But I don't have time to think of a response, because he buries his face in my snatch.

His tongue is magic. It can be hard, driving against my clit without a hint of mercy. It can be soft, licking my pussy lips like they're the most exotic ice cream ever made.

He does things with his mouth I can't define, and his teeth, too. He's drinking me, eating me, consuming every inch of me, and I'm soaring, soaring, soaring, until he delivers a single, devastating tap to my clit with his thumb.

I collapse in on myself. I clutch and clutch and clutch. My knees slam tight, keeping Trap's face deep in my pussy, and he rides the wild tide, fucking me with his tongue as I come until I cannot see.

It seems like centuries before I return to my body. I can hear my breath, long, deep pulls that do their best to anchor me. I can smell sex, my pussy's briny scent mixed with good, clean sweat. I can see the ceiling above me, and if I tilt my head, the wall of windows, black against the night outside.

My legs are trembling, still clamped shut to lock in the final, stuttering waves of my orgasm. I feel the weight of Trap's face against me, the soft lap of his tongue as he drinks my final shudders.

"Oh my God!" I make my knees open. "Did I hurt you? I'm so sorry!"

He pushes himself up on his elbows, eying me over my shaved mound. His face glistens, soaked by my juices. "I'm not," he says. His kisses along the inside of my thigh make me giggle.

Me. Giggle.

This is *fun*. I know I told Trap I want him to fuck me next, but I've changed my mind. I'm adding to the menu.

I scramble to my knees, feeling the stretch and sigh of muscles that I know will be sore tomorrow. With hands that seem to have taken lessons on their own, I push Trap down to the bed. I slip my fingers under the elastic of his boxers until I've pulled them past his feet. I crouch between his legs and watch his cock rise in eager greeting.

When I cup his balls, I'm surprised by their weight. I worry about crushing them, about hurting him, but I remember the pressure he placed on my hand as he led me over his body. He grunts as I gather the sack in one tight hand and squeeze.

I use my fingernails to trace the veins on his cock. He gets harder as I learn him. Longer too. "Sweet Jesus fuck," he says when I measure the rim beneath his even more sensitive tip.

He tapped my clit and I came. I wonder if I can do the same to him, tease him, tap him, play him to the end. But it's not enough to touch him. I want to taste him, too.

I need him in my mouth. His cock is too long for me to take the whole thing. I close my lips over the rounded end, sliding down until he hits the back of my throat. My eyes water, and I start to gag, so I pull up, tightening my lips to make up for the lack of depth.

His fists tangle in my hair, pulling hard enough for me to know he wants me, but not enough to hurt. I use my own hands to tickle his balls, and he almost slips out of my mouth when he leaps in surprise.

We find our rhythm—short, sharp darts of my head, taking him as deep as I can, then long, slow pulls as I draw back to his tip. He talks the entire time—encouragement at first, then beautiful, filthy words about how I look swallowing his cock.

I stretch my neck, managing the deepest thrust yet, and his fingers tighten on the back of my neck. I freeze, terrified I've done something wrong. "One more like that," he says through gritted teeth, "and you won't get the rest of the show."

I want to feel him come inside my mouth—pulsing and hot, shooting down my throat with the pearly ropes he painted on me hours ago. But I want to feel him fuck me, even more.

I take my time rising off his beautiful cock, relaxing my lips and easing my fingers from his balls. He has more control than I feared, or he purposely stopped me early. As I sit back, he groans and fumbles for something on the nightstand.

I'd forgotten about the condoms he showed me ages ago. For just a moment, I hesitate, wondering if he expects me to put one on him. I've never done that, and I don't want to do it wrong. I don't want to hurt him. I don't want to ruin everything we've got.

He tears the foil with steady fingers and takes out the round of rubber. He rolls it onto his sturdy erection the way he does everything else—with absolute, unshakeable certainty. His quick glance lets me know he wants me to see, wants me to learn.

When he's good and wrapped, he pulls me close for a kiss. His hand spreads across the back of my head, fingers twining in my hair. His lips are hard on mine, asking, promising, demanding. When I open to him, his tongue meets mine, and a satisfied rumble rises from his chest.

When we come up for air, he pulls away. I'd whimper, complain, but his hands are on my tits now. He squeezes them hard, just the way I asked him to, and then he closes his lips over the tight, hard peak of my right nip.

I squeal at the pressure. He laughs, but he doesn't let me go, brushing me with his teeth. He switches to the other tit, squeezing, sucking hard, and the pressure of his tongue almost makes me come.

He edges a knee between mine, making room for his body. He matches his hips to mine, letting me feel his weight. He rises up on one hand, using the other to bring the tip of his cock to the soaking wet lips of my pussy.

"Ready?" he asks, and I don't trust myself with words, but I nod.

He eases in, steady and slow.

I stretch around him, hovering on the point of pain. I tilt my hips and find a better angle. My breath catches because I've never felt this full.

He brushes the hair off my face. He tells me I'm his good

girl, his beautiful girl, that I can take this. He settles home, and the tight curls above his cock tease my sensitive, shaved mound.

And then he starts to move.

Slowly at first, raising his hips. He's leaving me, pulling away. I ache with emptiness even before he's gone. But then he pushes back, sliding home faster, deeper, even though I thought I'd already taken all he has to give.

Once he sets the rhythm, I instinctively rise to meet him. My body knows this dance, or it learns as we go.

Faster.

Harder.

More.

My toes stretch to needy points. My thighs tighten into desperate steel. My eyes close and my breath stalls and I need need need…

His fingers flash between us, scissoring around the hot tight pearl of my clit. He flicks once and a fuse sizzles through my body. Fire sparks up my spine and detonates in my brain at the same time my cunt explodes.

I thought I'd found nirvana the first time I came in this bed. But now I'm carried to an entirely different universe. Now, my muscles tighten *around* Trap's velvet cock. The sensations inside me multiply, echo around themselves until I don't know if I'm coming or screaming or begging or crying and the perfect spiral goes on and on and on.

Just when I think I can't take any more, that I have to faint or disappear or explode in a cloud of glittery dust, Trap drives home one last time. His chest pins mine, his legs anchor mine, his arms press against mine as every muscle in his body turns to stone.

I feel him pulse inside me, the rush of liquid heat as he comes. He bellows against my shoulder; his teeth clenching until I know they'll leave a mark. I hold him as he bucks, as he strains, until the aftershocks finally fade to a feather-like tremble.

"Ella…" he sighs, pulling out and rolling off to lie beside me on the bed. His dangling hand brushes my tit; he rolls his fingers over my nip, but my nerves have fired past the point of any response.

I'm drifting toward sleep when I feel him push off the bed. He pads into the bathroom. Water runs, and he comes back with a washcloth. He wipes between my legs gently, and my spent body registers nothing but soft warmth. He eases a pillow beneath my head.

My brain is stripped, its gears left in melting pieces. I know there's something I need to say, something I need to do, but when I try to string together words, Trap mumbles a kiss against my temple.

"Sleep," he says, the single word little more than a sighing breath.

That's not what he said in the kitchen. That wasn't the deal we made. Trap Prince never lets a woman spend the night. He told me that.

But he's told me so many things tonight, taught me so much more than I ever thought I could learn.

So I close my eyes.

I sink deep into my pillow.

I sleep.

20

ALIX

I startle awake, sitting up like someone rammed a cattle prod against my tongue. For just a moment, I don't know where I am, but then I see the wall of windows, the endless bed, the leather cuffs still fastened to the iron uprights. The entire night floods back into my brain.

Trap is sleeping beside me. He's sprawled on his back, legs splayed, one hand over his head. His tired cock rests against his thigh. I don't know how long we've been out, but given his utter exhaustion, I don't think it's been long.

As I shift to the edge of the bed, he mutters my name.

"Go back to sleep," I say. "I'm getting a drink."

He mumbles something, but he's out before he manages actual words.

There's a glass on the nightstand. I could get my drink in the bathroom, but I've already woken Trap once. After the night he's just had—the physical, but the emotional too—he deserves every second of sleep he can steal.

I slip into my panties before I realize there's no way I can put on my dress without disturbing the sleeping man. I settle for pulling on his boxers and his soft black T-shirt. I collect my dress and my bra to put on downstairs, snagging my shoes for good measure. I tip-toe down the stairs and into the kitchen.

I'm about to search the cabinets for a glass when I glance at the stove. A clock glows balefully in the moonlight from the wall of windows. 11:32.

Crap!

Everything rushes back to me—Leo missing our birthday and the eviction notice and my midnight deadline before I lose everything I own. For one blinding moment, I think about running up the stairs, about startling Trap from sleep and begging him to drive me home.

Before I can move, though, a wave of shame washes over me, so intense I almost retch in the sink. My life is an absolute mess. If there's something to do wrong, I've done it. I've got no family. No friends. No degree in sight. All because of a brother who has lied and lied and lied again.

But I've learned something tonight, in the magical world of Diamond Freeport. I've learned how to use my words.

I'm going home right now. I'm telling Leo I don't want to hear his excuses. I don't care why he blew off our birthday lunch. He can get clean on his own. Get a job on his own. Prove he's worth me on his own.

I'm through twisting my life for Leo.

And tomorrow, when I've said all the things I need to say, when I've said the words I've swallowed for far too long, I'll tell Trap what he's really done for me. I'll explain what tonight really meant.

Because then I'll be worthy. Then I'll deserve to be with him.

I glance at the clock again. 11:36.

I grab my clutch, where I left it on the counter hours ago. My phone is waiting.

No Uber, no Lyft, because Leo's kept me from having a credit card for years. But I've still got ten crisp twenties in my bag, the last from the ATM. I tap a stored number for Dover Yellow Cab.

They say they can be here in ten minutes. I beg them to hurry and hang up the call. Only then do I realize I have seven voice messages.

I tap the red badge and see they're all from Leo. He's going to beg me. He's going to lie. I delete all seven without listening.

He's left me texts, too. Nine of them. I have to scroll through those to delete, and I glimpse his growing panic.

Sorry about lunch

Hope u didnt wait 2 long

Can we talk

Al - got 2 talk

Call me

Rlly need 2 talk now

Come on Al

Im not kidding

ALIX

I jam my phone back in my clutch and gather my belongings. I look around the kitchen, but there isn't a scrap of paper anywhere.

I pad into the office, figuring even a Prince living in an ultra-modern castle has to have a pen where he works. I'm halfway to the desk when I hear the double-tap of a car horn.

The gate!

I've completely forgotten the iron gate. The cab dispatcher must have heard the urgency in my voice and gotten a car here faster than the ten minutes she quoted.

Forgetting the note I want to leave, I juggle my clothes, throwing the lock on the front door.

The car honks again.

"Ella?" Trap calls from the bedroom.

What was I thinking? Why didn't I just wake him and ask him to drive me home?

But the cab is waiting, and my keycard will die in twenty minutes and my phone is filled with my brother's incoherent rambling, the very thing I didn't want to explain to Trap.

I throw the door open and run across the driveway, in front of the office building, past the construction site. The cab is waiting by the front gate, its headlights slicing through the night.

My bare feet scrape against the paving stones. Ground lights flare to life behind me, outlining the driveway.

"Ella!" Trap calls again from the house's front door, louder, more commanding.

The cab starts to pull away. I scream, "Wait!" and break into an all-out run.

I start to drop my clutch, scramble for it, and my dress begins to drag. I bunch it into a ball, crushing my bra, and one of my shoes falls.

I start to go back for it, but the cab is leaving, so I forget about the shoe and fling myself at the gate. It takes me a moment to find the revolving door, the curved metal that will let me out while keeping any invader from breaking in.

I stumble into the road, three feet in front of the cab, and I'm blinded by its headlights.

"Ella!" Trap hollers, somewhere to my left.

"I'm sorry!" I call into the darkness. "I didn't mean…" I can't remember what I did or didn't mean. "I have to…" I can't explain everything I have to do. "I'm sorry," I shout again. "I'll call you! I promise!"

I stagger to the cab and yank open the door. Tumbling into the back seat, I tell the driver my address, and I beg him to get me home by midnight.

21

ALIX

∾

11:57.

I give the cabbie a massive tip because I can't wait for change. I slam my keycard against the reader, half expecting it to refuse to open. It takes three tries, but the door finally buzzes, and I tumble into the lobby like a boxer collapsing on the ropes. As always, it stinks like pizza and gym socks.

For once, I'm grateful the metal panels in the elevator are too dented and scarred to cast back a reflection. I swipe at my eyes, not certain when I started to cry. I bend down and wipe my nose with the hem of Trap's shirt.

I've made a huge mistake. I should have stayed with Trap. Should have trusted him. Should have explained. I acted like Alix, a woman afraid to use her words, afraid to tell the truth. I should have been Ella.

He would have understood.

My brain was paralyzed by the thought of losing everything

I own as the clock struck twelve. But I should have realized nothing in my lousy apartment is worth what I left behind.

As soon as I'm inside, I'll call him. How hard can it be to track down a number for Diamond Freeport? I'll say I made a mistake. I'll take the blame and beg him for a do-over. I'll offer to meet him at Debasement. Whatever he wants. Whatever he needs.

My key sticks in the lock, but I know exactly where to kick the door and how hard to shove with my shoulder. I slam it shut behind me.

"Alix!"

Leo sits on the swayback couch. His pillow and sheets must still be in the closet. He hasn't set up his bed for the night.

"Leo," I say, trying to keep my tone even.

"Didn't you get my messages?" he asks. "I left them on your phone."

He's nervous, glancing over my shoulder, looking at his hands, keeping his gaze from anywhere but me.

"I deleted your calls," I say. It feels good to speak the truth.

"You shouldn't have done that," he says. His voice shakes, and I wonder when he last used.

"There's a lot of things I shouldn't have done." I know precisely what I want to say and how I want to say it, but the words are still hard. I've held them back for so many years. I clutch my clothes to my chest.

"I'm sorry," Leo says, the two words blurring together.

"I'm sorry, too," I say. "I'm sorry you didn't tell me about the eviction sooner. I'm sorry you didn't—"

"No!" Leo cuts me off. "This is important!"

"I know. It's always important. You didn't mean to start using again. You thought you could handle just one hit. You didn't know you were slipping until you fell—"

"I tried!"

"You always try!"

"You're not listening to me!" He's sobbing now, frantic.

I've always been the one person who understands. I've always been the one person who believes him. I've loved him. He's my twin.

"I'm through listening to you," I say, trying to make my voice gentle. "You need help, Leo. A lot more help than I can give you."

"Please!" he cries, dropping to his knees. He waddles across the floor, hands clasped in front of his chest, like a bad movie's stereotype of a man with nothing left to lose.

Despite everything, I'm crying again. I've always wanted to protect him. Always wanted to make him whole.

"You've been to enough meetings," I say, even though he's gasping so hard I doubt he can hear me. "You know how this works. Maybe if you actually reach rock bottom, you can finally—"

"No!" he cries, and I suddenly remember a day when we were eight years old. We took kites to the Washington Monument, and his caught an updraft. The kite swept high above the obelisk, stretching, straining, until the end of the string slipped free of the spool and it was gone forever.

Leo screamed then the way he just screamed now. Like he's losing everything in the world.

I don't want to wake the neighbors. I glance over my shoulder to make sure the door is closed.

For a second, I can't parse what I'm seeing. A man stands there, a stranger. He's wearing black jeans and a black T and his hands are covered by jet black gloves. He could be Trap, but he isn't.

He's shorter than Trap. He's got acne on his cheeks, angry red pits, and his lips cave in like he's missing most of his teeth. His muddy brown eyes are dead.

I open my mouth to scream, but he gets an arm around my throat, yanking my head back against his shoulder. I twist and try to knee him in the balls, but he anticipates me and jerks me off my feet.

"Leo!" I scream—or try to. The sound is cut off by the arm crushing my larynx.

"Get the hood, motherfucker," the man snarls. I thrash like a dying fish, trying to see his accomplice. I land an elbow in my guy's ribs, and he huffs like a wild boar. "Let's go, cocksucker—the hood!" And then, wheezing, stinking like onion: "Don't make me go for my knife."

I turn toward Leo, trying to warn him. I don't know if he heard the part about the knife.

But Leo doesn't need a warning.

Leo is standing in front of me.

Leo is sobbing like the day Fluffy McFluffster went to kitty heaven.

Leo is holding a rough burlap sack, his hands shaking so hard I think he's going to drop it.

"I'm sorry," he babbles. "I'm so, so sorry. I owe him so much money. He said he was going to kill me. He said he'll only keep you a few days. You'll be okay. He promised. I made him promise, Alix. I did!"

He puts the hood over my head like we're going trick-or-treating, his hands shaking so hard he can barely pull it past my eyes. The guy behind me uses his free hand to yank it down harder, muttering, "Fucking junkie pussy."

"Oh my God, Leo," I gasp, because jerking the hood loosened the guy's hold on my throat. "What did you do?"

I ask the question, but he's already told me. With diamond-sharp clarity, I'm certain: the brother I love has just sold me to pay his drug debts.

Before I can beg, I feel a sting like a fist-size hornet launching an attack on my neck. It must be a needle, because my blood turns to fire, torching a path from my neck, down my arm, to my heart.

I open my mouth to scream, but I'm gone before I can force out a sound.

~

I hope you enjoyed reading *Diamond Solitaire.* My love story with Trap Prince continues in *Rough Diamond,* the next book in the now-complete Kidnapped Series.

Buy *Rough Diamond* Now!
https://alixkey.com/PB1US

MORE DIAMOND RING

~

Looking for an Irish Mob retelling of Jane Eyre? *Irish Brute*, the true love story of Braiden Kelly and Samantha Mott, is a Kindle Unlimited read.Start the Irish Mob Series by typing

https://alixkey.com/KI4US

into your phone or computer browser.

~

One last thing: If you want an absolutely free full-length, totally stand-alone Diamond Ring novel, featuring a gender-switch Jack and the Beanstalk retelling and starring Irish mobster Connor Boyle, I've got you covered! Just type:

https://alixkey.com/sins

into your phone or computer browser.

THANK YOU

I can't thank you enough for choosing *Diamond Solitaire* from among all the dark romances out there! Without readers like you, I would never have my writing career.

You may not realize it, but *you* can be my hero. Study after study shows that the number one reason a person reads a book is because that book was recommended by a friend.

So will you tell one friend about *Diamond Solitaire*?

Of course, if you're dead-set on reviewing my book on Amazon and Goodreads, I won't complain! Honest reviews are hugely helpful because many advertisers require me to have a certain number of reviews before I can buy ads.

Leave a review on Amazon
https://alixkey.com/KI0US

Leave a review on Goodreads
https://alixkey.com/GR0

Whatever you do, don't be a stranger! I look forward to hearing from you soon!

www.alixkey.com
alix@alixkey.com

ABOUT THE AUTHOR

Alix Key was born in Potomac, Maryland, where she grew up making her twin brother and all her dolls act out her favorite fairytales. When an all-grown-up Alix discovered that very real dangers lurk in the woods, she figured out how to rescue herself. She now lives outside Dover, Delaware with her own Prince Charming. When not writing dark romance, Alix serves as the Chief Operations Officer of Diamond Freeport.

You can learn more about Alix at her website, www.alixkey.com.